"I think a change of scene to a safe environment could speed the emotional healing process. And Oak Hill is about as safe a small town as you get," Sam said.

"Okay. I'll come."

A surge of elation washed over him, but he did his best to maintain his composure. "Good. Will you be okay making the trip alone?"

"I'll manage."

"Okay. I'll look forward to seeing you, Cara." Try as he might, Sam couldn't keep a hint of warmth from creeping into his voice.

"I'll be in touch." Without waiting, Cara hung up. It suddenly occurred to her that she hadn't thanked him for his invitation. Her visit might be precisely what she needed to start her on the road to recovery, but it could also turn out to be a disaster. She'd just have to put the outcome in God's hands.

And pray she hadn't made the biggest mistake of her life.

Books by Irene Hannon

Love Inspired

*Home for the Holidays #6
*A Groom of Her Own #16
*A Family To Call
    Her Own #25
It Had To Be You #58
One Special Christmas #77
The Way Home #112
Never Say Goodbye #175
Crossroads #224
†The Best Gift #292
†Gift from the Heart #307

†The Unexpected Gift #319
All Our Tomorrows #357
The Family Man #366
Rainbow's End #379
‡From This
    Day Forward #419

*Vows
†Sisters & Brides
‡Heartland Homecoming

IRENE HANNON

An author of more than twenty-five novels, Irene Hannon is a prolific writer whose books have been honored with both a coveted RITA® Award from Romance Writers of America and a Reviewer's Choice Award from *Romantic Times BOOKreviews* magazine.

A former corporate communications executive with a Fortune 500 company, she now devotes herself full-time to writing. Her emotionally gripping books feature hope-filled endings that highlight the tremendous power of love and faith to transform lives.

In her spare time Irene performs in community musical theater productions and is a church soloist. Cooking, gardening, reading and spending time with family are among her favorite activities. She and her husband make their home in Missouri—a preferred setting for many of her novels!

Irene invites you to visit her Web site at www.irenehannon.com.

From This Day Forward
Irene Hannon

Steeple
Hill®

Published by Steeple Hill Books™

STEEPLE HILL BOOKS

Steeple Hill®

ISBN-13: 978-0-373-87455-2
ISBN-10:   0-373-87455-3

FROM THIS DAY FORWARD

Copyright © 2007 by Irene Hannon

Printed in U.S.A.

The Lord is close to the brokenhearted;
and those who are crushed in spirit he saves.
—*Psalms* 33:18

To Tom
My very own heartland hero!

Chapter One

"Sam, it's Liz. I need to speak with you right away. Call me on my cell."

A jolt of adrenaline shot through Sam Martin as he set his black medical bag on the kitchen counter and reached for the pad and pen next to the answering machine. He hadn't seen Liz Warren, his wife's best friend, since the night Cara left him, and he'd only spoken with her once after that. If she was calling, something was up. And a sick feeling of dread told him it wasn't good.

Jotting down the number as she recited it, Sam checked his watch. If his house call deep in rural Missouri hadn't taken two hours, he would have arrived back in Oak Hill early enough to return the call without guilt. But it was almost eleven on the east coast, and Liz hadn't used the emergency cell phone number he provided on his home and office answering machines. Whatever she wanted to talk to him about couldn't be urgent. But there was no way he could wait until tomorrow to find out the reason for her call. Better to risk waking her than spend a sleepless night counting the hours until morning.

As he punched in Liz's number, it occurred to him that she might have gone out for the evening. It was Saturday, after all. But if she had, he'd leave a message to call him back when she returned, no matter the hour. He'd be awake anyway.

To his relief, a live voice answered. "Hello."

"Liz, it's Sam. I just got your message."

There was a slight hesitation before she responded. "I've been having some second thoughts about calling you."

Sam heard the coolness—and caution—in her voice. No surprise there. She'd been Cara's best friend far longer than he'd known his wife. And she'd witnessed his ultimate betrayal. He understood—and respected—her loyalty. But he wasn't about to hang up without finding out why she'd called. It was too late for that.

"I assume it concerns Cara."

Another brief silence.

"Look, Sam, to be honest, you're the last person I wanted to call," Liz finally said. "If Cara's parents weren't on a missionary trip in Africa for a year, and if her sister wasn't eight months pregnant and in the middle of preparing to move, I'd have called them. But they are and she is, so I didn't know who else to contact."

"About what, Liz?" Sam's grip on the phone tightened. It took every ounce of his restraint to remain calm when his mind was racing with terrifying scenarios.

"I…I think Cara needs some help. I've tried to talk with her about it, but she shuts me out and says she's fine. Except she isn't. Not even close. And I don't know what else to do." Her voice broke on the last word.

"Okay, Liz, you're going to have to back up. What's wrong with Cara? Is she sick?" Sam couldn't stop the quiver that ran through his voice. Liz was the most in-control woman he'd ever met. If she was upset enough to let her emotions show, there was a major problem.

"Not physically." The sound of a deep breath being drawn came over the line. When she continued, she sounded more like herself. "A month ago, Cara and another chef named Tony were leaving the restaurant after hours, and they were accosted in the parking lot by a robber. When Tony tried to resist, the guy shot him. He died before the ambulance got there."

A muscle in Sam's jaw clenched. Cara had witnessed a murder—and possibly faced death herself. If he hadn't made a mess of their marriage, he'd have been there for her through this trauma. Instead, she'd had to deal with it—and the aftermath—alone.

"Tell me…" He stopped and cleared his throat, then tried again. "Tell me about Cara."

"She tried to go back to work a few days after the shooting, but when she had a panic attack in the kitchen the owner suggested she take a little time off. The thing is, though, she's not getting any better. She rarely leaves her apartment, and never at night. She's anxious in the dark and can't sleep when she's by herself. She has persistent nightmares. I found that out when she stayed with us at the beginning. But now she thinks she's wearing out her welcome…as if that was possible! Anyway, I know she's still not sleeping."

Post-traumatic stress disorder. It was an easy diagnosis, but a difficult condition to treat. Sam had learned enough about it in the past couple of years to write a book. "Does her family know about any of this?"

"No. She said they all have enough on their plates, and since she wasn't hurt there was no need to upset them."

That sounded like Cara. She'd always put other people's needs above her own. The best example of that was when she'd stood by him after his own trauma, despite the verbal abuse he'd heaped on her. Perhaps now he could return the favor by being there for her as she had been for him. If she'd let him.

"I'll help in any way I can, Liz. What did you have in mind?" If he followed his instincts, he'd jump on the next plane to Philadelphia and show up at her door. Except she'd probably slam it in his face.

"I do have an idea. But it may not be convenient for you."

Based on his history, Liz's comment was fair. Sam knew he'd been selfish and self-absorbed and far too egotistical in the past. But things had changed. "That won't be an issue."

She mulled that over for a few seconds. "Okay. But it all hinges on whether or not you're…involved… with anyone."

The comment was like a slap. "I'm still married to Cara, Liz."

"Yeah. I know."

But that didn't stop you before.

She didn't have to say the words. Sam heard them anyway. His neck grew warm, and his mouth settled into a grim line. "There isn't anyone else, Liz. There never really was."

"Right." Without giving him a chance to respond to her sarcasm, she continued. "So what kind of living arrangement do you have there?"

"What do you mean?"

"House, apartment, condo?"

"House."

"Good. Okay, here's what I'm thinking. Cara needs somewhere safe to stay for a while, far away from the city. If you have room for her—and I mean that literally, as in a private room of her own—I think a small-town atmosphere in the heartland would be a perfect place for her to recover. But the last thing she needs is for someone to make her feel that she's imposing. Nor could she handle anger—for any reason. She needs understanding and security and safety."

Turning toward the window, Sam stared out into the darkness. Twelve years ago, when he and Cara married, he'd planned to give her all those things. But the image of her white, shocked face and shattered expression on that fateful night sixteen months ago reminded him how badly he'd failed. It was seared into his brain, the memory still powerful enough to clench his gut. To leave the bitter tang of regret on his tongue. To compel him to find a way to fix the damage and start anew, just as his skilled hands had once given his patients new life through surgery.

Maybe this was his chance.

"I can give her those things, Liz. And more."

His quiet, intense response seemed to surprise his

wife's best friend. "Okay. I'm already going to be in the doghouse for calling you. I can live with that if my idea helps her. But not if I end up sending her to a situation worse than the one she's in."

Although he knew Liz had a poor opinion of him, that comment rankled. "I'm not a monster. And despite what you might believe, I still love Cara. Yes, I made some mistakes. Bad ones—which I'll regret as long as I live. But people do change. I promise you that while Cara is here, I'll do everything I can to help her recover. No one wants that more than me. I have three bedrooms, and one of them is empty. She's welcome to stay as long as she wants to."

"*If* you can convince her to come. And that's a big if."

"I'll find a way."

His conviction seemed to impress Liz. A slight, almost imperceptible warmth crept into her voice. "I hope you do, Sam. Good luck."

With a troubled expression, Sam hung up the phone and pushed through the screen door to his back porch. The warmth of the early June evening was pleasant, with none of the mugginess that characterized typical Missouri nights later in the summer. A clear sky promised a fair tomorrow, the stars bright overhead, the moon full. The scent of honeysuckle wafted through the still night air, sweet and fresh. At the back of the property, a slight breeze whispered in the woods, and the faint echo of a steady whistle sounded as a distant train moved purposefully toward its destination.

The peaceful setting did little to calm Sam's roiling emotions, however. An hour ago, as he'd driven home through the dense night, he'd been no closer to a solution to his dilemma with Cara than he had been more than a year before, when she'd left him. Now an opportunity had been dropped in his lap.

But at Cara's expense.

Closing his eyes, Sam forced himself to take a deep, steadying breath as he tried to sort out his feelings. He could identify anger in the volatile mix. Directed at the perpetrator of a crime that had cost one man his life and scarred his wife psychologically. Guilt was jumbled in there, too. If he hadn't messed things up, he would have been there for Cara during this crisis. And there was also a healthy dose of compassion. No one understood the horror and trauma of the situation Cara had experienced better than him. He'd been there. He could empathize, and he wanted to help.

But the main reason he wanted her to come to Missouri was far simpler than that. He still loved her. As far as he was concerned, that alone justified her visit.

Yet Liz was right. Convincing Cara of that wasn't going to be easy. They'd had almost no direct communication since the night she'd left him, nor had he seen her. The sale of their condo had been handled by a real estate firm, business and financial matters by lawyers. When he'd tried to call her, he'd always gotten her answering machine. The flowers and cards he'd sent in the first few months had gone unacknowledged. It was clear that she wanted no contact with him.

And Sam didn't have a clue how to change her mind. His surgical skill had been almost intuitive. He was far less able when it came to matters of the heart. As the months had slipped by, his hopes for a reconciliation had dimmed. Yet he'd clung to them as fiercely as a drowning man clasps a life preserver, unable to accept that his marriage was over.

He'd been desperate enough to even consider asking God for help. But whatever tenuous connection he'd once felt with the Almighty had been severed by the tragic events that had robbed him of the career he prized and the woman he loved. In the end, turning to God for assistance hadn't been an option.

But now that an unexpected opportunity had been dropped into his lap, he wasn't going to let it slip away. If he couldn't convince Cara by phone to come, he'd fly to Philadelphia and camp on her doorstep. According to Liz, she needed help. And he intended to give it to her.

Nevertheless, he acknowledged the validity of Liz's final comment. He would need a lot of luck to pull this off. And maybe something more.

Maybe he needed God after all.

It had been years since Sam had prayed with any real conviction or sincerity. When he and Cara had married, his faith had been a matter of going through the motions. He'd been arrogant enough in the old days to think he didn't need the Almighty. Given his past conceit and lack of piousness, he doubted he was even on the Lord's radar screen anymore.

But this might be the only chance he got to reconnect with his wife, and he was going to need all the help he could get—not only to convince Cara to come to Oak Hill, but to help restore a sense of normalcy to her life. He couldn't blow it.

Raising his gaze to the star-studded sky, he sent a silent plea heavenward.

Lord, if You're listening, I want You to know that I'm not asking for Your help for me, but for Cara. Please show me how to reach her. Open her heart to my invitation so that I can help her overcome her fear and regain her trust. Much as I want to rebuild our relationship, it's more important right now for her to heal. And if that's all I can accomplish, Lord, then please...help me put aside my own selfish needs and accept that it's enough. But if You can see Your way to let me win back her love, I would be forever grateful.

Chapter Two

"Cara, if you're there, please pick up. It's important."

Shocked, Cara stared at her answering machine. Although Sam hadn't identified himself, nor had he called in quite a while, years could go by—decades, even—and she'd recognize his mellow, resonant voice. She'd always liked the way it sounded first thing in the morning, husky from sleep and oh-so-appealing.

And it was definitely first thing in the morning in Missouri, she confirmed, checking the clock on her kitchen counter. Six o'clock, in fact. He must have rung her as soon as he got up. Not that the early hour mattered. Sleeping at night was next to impossible. Every little sound seemed magnified—and threatening—in the dark.

"Cara, are you there?"

With a start, she realized that he was still on the line, waiting to see if she'd pick up. Well, he'd find out soon enough she wasn't going to. Let him leave a message if it was that important.

"Okay, I'm hanging up. But I plan to keep calling until we connect."

As the line went dead, his last word echoed in her mind. *Connect.* How ironic that he would use that term, Cara mused, her shoulders collapsing in a weary slump as she leaned back against the countertop. They hadn't connected in years. Not since their careers had taken off and their lives had gone in different directions.

And she was as much to blame for their drifting apart as he was, she acknowledged. She'd been just as ambitious as Sam, just as driven to excel at her profession. She'd worked until late at night. He'd been gone when she got up in the morning. Weekends, when he had a few spare minutes, were her busiest days. So he filled them with more work. And little by little he'd become more distracted as the demands of his surgical career mushroomed and his prestige grew. Busy with her own career as a chef, Cara hadn't noticed the widening gulf between them—until the year he'd forgotten their anniversary. Worse, he hadn't seemed to care.

His indifference had hurt. And it had served as a wake-up call for her. After praying about it and considering a number of options, Cara had waited for a night when Sam came home early. Once she'd had his attention, she'd laid her proposal on the table: She would take a job with more reasonable hours in a lesser-known restaurant if he would reduce his patient caseload to allow them to spend more time together. While such a radical change would require sacrifices, she'd been convinced that it would be worth it to save their marriage.

Not only had he refused to consider her suggestion, he'd plunged more deeply into his work.

That was when she'd known they were in big trouble.

In time, perhaps she would have found another way to salvage their relationship, Cara reflected. But then tragedy had struck, leaving Sam crippled in both body and spirit. Told he would never operate again, he'd made her the target of his bitterness. Sustained by prayer, she could have endured even that, clinging to the hope that a brighter day would dawn. But when confronted by the evidence of his ultimate betrayal, that hope had died. Devastated, she'd tucked the fragments of love that remained for him deep in her heart and moved on with her life. It hadn't been easy, but she'd coped.

Until a month ago.

Closing her eyes, Cara drew an unsteady breath. Thank God, she'd had Liz! Every time fear had started to choke her, Liz had helped her breathe. Every time the world began to crumble beneath her feet and she lost her balance, Liz had held out a steadying hand. Every time a panic attack gripped her, Liz had talked her through it. In the past month, her friend had changed her plans for Cara's sake more often than prices fluctuated at the gas pump.

Yet despite Liz's support, and much to Cara's surprise, it was often Sam who crept uninvited—and unwanted—into her thoughts. For the past month, the memories of their early days together had been vivid in her mind, days when a mere touch of his hand or one of his warm smiles could chase away her problems. And despite her best efforts, she'd been unable to squelch a powerful yearning for the secure, sheltering haven of his arms.

How odd that he would call now, when she felt more fragile and vulnerable than ever before. It was also dangerous, she warned herself. Sam wasn't the answer to her problems. He'd *been* the problem in the past. Rekindling the ashes of their long-dead relationship was not an option.

Pushing thoughts of the past aside, she reached for a mug from a hook above the counter. But as she grasped the cool ceramic handle, the sudden ringing of the phone startled her and her hand jerked. The mug slipped from her fingers, shattering on the unforgiving tile at her feet.

"Cara, it's Sam again. I'm going to keep calling until you answer. I need to talk with you. Please pick up."

Glancing from the jagged shards strewn across the floor to the clock, Cara struggled to regulate her breathing. He'd only waited ten minutes before calling back. Did he plan to keep this up all day? *Please, God, no!* Her nerves couldn't take it.

When the line went dead at last, Cara knelt and began to pick up the remnants of her favorite mug. As she collected the pieces, sudden tears stung her eyes and she swiped at them angrily. She wasn't going to cry about a stupid mug. She wasn't! She'd never been a weepy person. Even during the final difficult months with Sam, she'd never cried. Yet for the past four weeks, the smallest thing could trigger a flood of tears—further evidence of her unsettled emotional state. And she was tired of it! Tired of jumping at the slightest noise. Tired of feeling out of control.

But she didn't know how to break the cycle of fear. Even prayer, once such a steadying influence, hadn't been able to calm her. Still, she clung to the belief that things would return to normal. That, at some point, she'd be able to deal with the aftereffects of the trauma, go back to work, move on with her life. She *had* to believe that. Because she couldn't continue like this.

As she deposited the broken mug in the trash, the phone rang again. Once more Sam's voice echoed in the silent, empty room, leaving the same message.

Though her curiosity was piqued by his persistence, Cara steeled herself to his words. Eventually he'd tire of the game and leave a message. She could wait.

An hour later, after turning up the radio while she took a long, hot shower and blow-dried her hair, Cara returned to the kitchen to find the message light on her answering machine blinking, the number eight illuminated on the digital display. Meaning he'd called six times in the past sixty minutes. She replayed the messages, but they were all the same. None contained a clue about the purpose of his call.

After hitting the delete button, Cara was starting to turn away when the phone rang again. She was prepared to ignore it until Liz spoke.

"Hi, Cara. Sorry to call this early, but I figured you'd be up and—"

Lunging for the phone, Cara snatched it out of the cradle. "Liz? Sorry. I thought you were…someone else."

There was a momentary hesitation, and when Liz responded her tone was cautious. "Who?"

"You're not going to believe this." Cara perched on a stool by the counter. "Sam's been calling. Every ten minutes, starting about an hour and a half ago." When silence greeted her news, a puzzled frown creased Cara's brow. "Liz? Are you there?"

"Yeah, I'm here. Have you talked to him?"

"Of course not!"

"Did he leave a message?"

"Just that he needs to talk to me. And that he'll keep calling until I answer."

Silence again.

A tingle of suspicion began to niggle at the edges of Cara's consciousness, and her grip on the phone tightened. "Liz? Do you know something about this?"

The heavy sigh that came over the line gave Cara her answer even before Liz spoke. "Look, Cara, I'm sorry. I've been so worried about you…I didn't know who else to call, since your family was off-limits."

It took a few seconds for Liz's meaning to register. But only a heartbeat more for Cara's disbelief to morph into anger—and accusation. "You called Sam?"

"I thought he could help. You need to get away from here, Cara. Sam lives in a small town in the heartland. He has an extra room in his house. You'd be safe there."

"I can't believe this! What did you tell him?" Cara's voice rose, shrill and bordering on hysteria, as she vaulted to her feet.

"Just the basics of what happened. Cara, I'm sorry. I didn't know what else to do."

There was a trace of tears in Liz's words, but Cara ignored her friend's distress, clamping her lips shut.

"You can't go back to work, you don't sleep, you have nightmares, you won't go out at night." Liz laid out her case in the stony silence that hung on the line. "I have to drag you out of the apartment even in the daylight. That's not normal."

The truth of Liz's words did nothing to ease Cara's anger. How could Liz do this to her? Of all people, Liz knew how Cara felt about her husband. Her friend had witnessed the incident that had delivered the fatal blow to their marriage. As far as Cara was concerned, the only difference between the two betrayals was that Liz's intentions had been good. But as conventional wisdom was fond of pointing out, the road to a certain undesirable location was paved with those.

"I saw a murder." Cara choked on the word, and her fingers clenched around the phone. "It takes time to recover from trauma like that."

"Sometimes it also takes professional help. But you won't consider that."

That was true, Cara conceded. She'd always been a strong person, and she'd been convinced she could work through the aftermath of the attack on her own. But the depth and power of her trauma had overwhelmed her. Despite her best efforts, she wasn't making any progress.

"Since you won't get professional help, a change of scene might be a good thing," Liz pressed, when Cara didn't reply. "What better place than small-town America, where people don't even feel a need to lock their doors? Sam has a spare bedroom in his house that he's willing to let you use. I think you should consider it."

"You can't be serious!"

"Yes, I am."

"You want me to live under the same roof with the

man who…" Cara stopped, too shocked by the absurdity of the suggestion to complete the thought.

"I know it's kind of awkward, but…"

"Awkward? That doesn't even come close to describing the scenario you're proposing!" Once more, a touch of hysteria sharpened Cara's voice.

"Okay, maybe this is weird. No, scratch that. It *is* weird," Liz admitted. "But as far as I'm concerned, the situation is desperate. The thing is, Cara, Sam can offer you a safe place to stay until you feel stronger. Think of it this way. He owes you after all he put you through. No matter how you feel about him, at least he'll be a warm body in the house at night so you can feel safe enough to sleep. And during the day, when he's at work, you'll have the place to yourself. It's a good plan. And Sam is willing."

"Why?"

"Why what?"

"Why is he willing?"

"Who knows? Guilt, maybe?" In truth, Liz thought it was more than that. But she wasn't about to share that intuition with Cara. Her friend would turn tail and run in the opposite direction if she suspected Sam had other—more personal—reasons for extending the invitation. "What does it matter? Just consider it a safe place to stay for a few weeks."

Safe, Cara reflected. That depended on your definition of the word. In a physical sense, Liz might be right. But given her precarious emotional state, and the too-prominent role Sam had played in her wayward musings this past month, Cara wasn't at all sure about the security of her heart. She'd have to constantly remind herself that she and Sam could never recapture the closeness they'd once shared. That there had been too many hurts, too much betrayal. If she went, she couldn't harbor any illusions. Sam's home would be a place to recuperate. Nothing more.

If she went.

A shock wave rippled through Cara. When had she started to even consider the trip an option? She groped for the counter and eased back onto the stool, suddenly shaky.

"Cara?" An uncertain note crept into Liz's voice. "Hey, I had your best interest at heart. I'm sorry if I made a mistake. You know how much our friendship means to me, and I was aware of the risk when I called Sam. But I couldn't figure out any other way to help you. Please don't hate me, okay?"

For fifteen years—since the day they'd met at a contemporary art exhibit both had been dragged to by their respective dates, only to find themselves laughing together in the ladies' room at the abstract, over-the-top junk that was being passed off as fine art—Liz had been like a second sister to Cara. Their friendship had been cemented long before either had married. How could she hold Liz's actions against her when she knew that her friend had been motivated by love?

"It's okay, Liz." Cara closed her eyes and took a slow, deep breath as she struggled to sort through her emotions. "This whole thing is just bizarre. Kind of like my life of late. I have to admit that I'm starting to feel a little like Job. But I've lost so much…I don't want to lose you, too. You saved my life this past month."

"Then you'll at least think about my idea?"

Propping her elbow on the counter, Cara pushed her hair back from her face and cupped her chin in her palm. She blinked, her eyes gritty with fatigue, as a shaft of bright morning light slanted through the window. Maybe a good night's sleep was reason enough to visit Sam.

"I'll pray about it, Liz."

"Sounds like a plan. And the sooner the better. I'll do the same."

As they hung up, Cara hoped Liz would honor her parting promise. Because this decision wouldn't be easy. And she was going to need all the guidance she could get.

Sam hit redial and checked his watch. He'd been at this phone game for three hours now, and Cara still wasn't answering. According to Liz, she rarely left her apartment, so he figured she was there—unless she'd gone to church. A good possibility, he realized, since regular worship was part of her routine. He could count on one hand the number of Sunday services she'd missed during their marriage.

The call went through, and Sam counted the rings. *One.* If she had gone to church, she should be home by now. *Two.* That meant she was ignoring him. *Three.* It looked like he might have to implement Plan B—get on a plane to Philadelphia and show up on her doorstep. *Four.*

Expecting the answering machine to kick in, he started to take a breath to leave a message when a live greeting came over the line. "Hello?"

The air whooshed out of his lungs.

"Hello?" Cara repeated when the silence lengthened.

He gulped in some oxygen. "Cara? It's Sam."

"I figured it might be." Her voice was as taut as a rubber band about to snap.

"Sorry about all the messages. It finally dawned on me that you must be at church."

"No."

His eyebrows rose. "You never miss."

"I've skipped the past few Sundays."

He didn't have to ask why. But if Cara was too nervous to go out even for services, Liz hadn't exaggerated his wife's trauma—or her need for help. Convincing her to let him provide it, however, was going to be a formidable challenge. He tried to think of some way to lead up to the purpose of his call, but in the end decided to plunge in. Why pretend that this was a normal conversation when they both knew it wasn't?

"I talked to Liz," he said without preamble.

"I know. She called me this morning."

Unsure whether that was good or bad, Sam tested the waters. "She told you about our conversation?"

"Yes."

When silence followed her single-word response, Sam realized that she wasn't going to make this easy for him. "I'm sorry for all you've been through, Cara."

Soft and caring, his comment took her off guard. It reminded her of the way he'd talked to her early in their marriage. Perhaps he'd learned a thing or two about empathy since their parting, Cara mused. She hoped so. For his sake.

"I survived." Her response came out a bit more curt than she intended, but maybe that was good. She didn't want Sam to think her feelings toward him had softened one iota during the months they'd been apart. Nor did she want to prolong this painful conversation.

He got the message. And got to the point. "Based on what Liz told me about your experience, I think her plan has merit. A change of scene, and a move to a safe environment, could speed the emotional healing process. I have a three-bedroom house, and one of the bedrooms is empty. You're welcome to use it for as long as you like."

Since her conversation with Liz, Cara had forced herself to consider the situation from a practical standpoint. And she'd done some intense praying. When she'd answered the phone, she'd been prepared to accept his offer.

But now that the moment had arrived, she hesitated. It had been one thing to decide on a course of action in the abstract, and another altogether to follow through when his warm, caring voice was already wreaking havoc with her unsettled emotions. If she reacted this way talking to him by phone, how in the world would she manage when she was living in his house?

Still, he'd be gone a great deal—working all day and well into the evening, if old patterns held. Their paths didn't have to cross that much. She had plenty of books she'd been wanting to read, and that could occupy her at night until he returned and she could go to sleep. It should be fine. Just because their marriage had fallen apart didn't mean they couldn't be adult enough to treat each other with civility for a few weeks.

"Okay."

Prepared to argue his case, Sam was taken aback by her easy acquiescence. "You're coming?" he clarified.

"Yes."

A surge of elation washed over him, but he did his best to maintain a steady tone as he responded. "Good. When?"

"I'm not sure. I'll make the arrangements and let you know."

"Will you be okay making the trip alone?"

"I'll manage."

Her reassurance didn't assuage his worry. He knew how debilitating panic attacks could be—as could the other symptoms of post-traumatic stress disorder. But he also knew that if he got too protective, she might back off. Even cancel her trip. And he couldn't risk that.

"Okay. I'll look forward to seeing you, Cara." Try as he might, he couldn't keep a touch of warmth from creeping into his voice. And her warning note when she responded told him she hadn't missed it.

"I'm only looking for a place to stay, Sam. Nothing more."

"Understood."

"I'll be in touch." Without waiting for him to reply, Cara hung up.

As she picked up a now-tepid cup of tea, it suddenly occurred to her that she hadn't thanked him for his invitation. Perhaps because she wasn't sure he was doing her any favors, she speculated. While her visit might be precisely what she needed to start her on the road to recovery, it could also turn out to be a disaster. Time would tell, she supposed. Until then, she'd just have to put the outcome in God's hands.

And pray she hadn't made the biggest mistake of her life.

Chapter Three

Wiping his hands on a damp rag, Sam reached for the can of soda balanced on the rungs of the ladder. As he took a long swallow, he gave the finished bedroom a satisfied survey. In the four days since Cara had agreed to come, he'd transformed the bland, beige room into an oasis. The walls were the exact shade of aquamarine his wife favored, and he'd given the dark woodwork three coats of semigloss white enamel to brighten up the space. Once he moved in the furniture, the bedroom would be a welcoming haven.

And he wanted his wife to feel welcome...even if he couldn't say the words.

A headache began to throb in his temples, and he moved to the window to raise the sash higher, hoping to lessen the smell of paint fumes. As he took in a deep breath of fresh air scented with new-mown grass, he recalled a conversation he'd had with Cara on their second date, after she'd teased him about his quietness.

"I was a home-schooled only child," he'd explained as

they strolled to his car after attending a concert. He'd been tempted to take her hand, but fear that she'd reject his overture had held him back. Instead, he'd stuck his hands in his pockets. "It was a very solitary upbringing. Mom was great at teaching me math and English and science, but I never had much opportunity to learn social skills."

"Oh, I don't know," she'd responded, her deep green eyes sparking with mischief as she tucked her hand through his arm with a natural ease he could only envy. "You may not be the smoothest talker I've ever met, but you managed to get me to go out with you."

"That was pure luck. Just like our meeting. If you hadn't given me a megawatt smile when you came over to our table that night at the request of my date, I don't think I would have had the guts to ask you out."

"It took a lot more dinners before you did. How many nights in a row did you eat at the restaurant? Six?"

"Ten. And I have the credit card bill to prove it."

"I'm sure your date rues the day she sent her compliments to the kitchen and insisted on meeting the chef." Cara had grinned at him.

"It was just a blind date, anyway."

"Are you serious?"

He'd felt her curious gaze and responded with a diffident shrug, hoping the lights from the shops they were passing weren't strong enough to illuminate his face. "Yes. A well-meaning coworker was determined to beef up my lackluster social life."

"You don't date much?"

"No."

"Hmm."

"What does that mean?" He'd been at a total loss about how to interpret her response. And in truth he hadn't been sure he wanted to. But her next words had reassured him.

"It means I'm honored you asked me out. I like you, Sam Martin. And as for the communication thing, we can work on that together, don't you think?"

He'd agreed, Sam recalled, as he downed the last of his soda and tapped the lid of the paint can back into place. He'd have agreed to almost anything Cara asked in those days, when the heady euphoria of new love had warmed his heart and added a dazzling brightness to his days.

But with thirteen years hindsight, he knew he hadn't held up his end of the bargain. When things had gotten tough, he'd reverted to old habits and shut down, destroying the marriage that had been the best thing in his life.

Gathering up the drop cloth and painting supplies, Sam gave the empty room one more swift scan. Soon it would be occupied by the woman he loved. Soon she would eat in his kitchen, walk through his garden, watch his television. Soon she would be back in his life.

And he intended to do everything in his power to convince her that that was where she belonged.

For always.

Flicking a glance in the rearview mirror, Cara edged into the exit lane on I-44 at Cuba, Missouri. So far, the drive had gone without a hitch. Not that she was surprised, given the brief but precise directions Sam had e-mailed her shortly after their phone conversation seven days ago. He had always been a stickler for accuracy, an attribute that had served him well as a surgeon, Cara reflected. His spare communication style, on the other hand, hadn't mattered a great deal in his medical specialty, given the limited interaction surgeons had with patients. But it wasn't good for establishing—or maintaining—relationships.

Recognizing that, Sam had made a concerted effort to be more communicative in the early days of their marriage, sharing both the events of his day and his feelings with her, even though that had been difficult for him. But later, as they'd grown apart, he'd gone back to his old ways, withdrawing into himself and sharing little of his life…and less of his emotions.

Once, Cara had believed she held the key to unlock his heart, that she could help him release the deeper feelings she knew were trapped inside. She'd tapped into them often enough to nourish her soul, to remind her that this often silent, solitary man loved her with an intensity that could take her breath away. Had their lives followed a different path, she felt sure they could have laid the groundwork for a solid marriage that would have endured.

But long before that foundation was established, life had intervened. Careers, commitments and demands had left neither of them with enough spare time or energy for the task. In the months preceding Sam's tragedy, they'd become less like loving spouses and more like strangers who lived under the same roof.

Fighting back a wave of melancholy, Cara forced herself to focus on the rural Missouri landscape around her on this mid-June Sunday. Rolling hills, green fields and forested knolls created a restful ambience that was a world removed from the hustle and bustle of Philadelphia—and from the stresses of her trip, which had been magnified a hundredfold by her unsettled emotions.

Oak Hill, and its quiet Main Street, offered yet another contrast to big-city life. A mere two blocks long, it reminded her of a Norman Rockwell painting, complete with soda fountain, feed store, single-screen movie theater and a homespun-looking café called Gus's.

She slowed as she approached the cross street at the end of the compact business district. Glancing to the left, she noted an elementary school, church, city hall and a few businesses tucked among residential properties. Swiveling her head the other way, she spotted a police station, newspaper office, more houses, a tiny library—and Sam's office.

This was it. He'd told her to turn here, pass his office, continue for another quarter mile, then make a left onto his street.

A sudden, familiar anxiety swept over her as she swung the wheel to the right, escalating with a rapidity that always frightened her. Since the robbery, she'd had these panic attacks far too often. In most cases, they struck for no reason. Today, however, she could pinpoint the cause: coming face-to-face with the man who had stolen her heart—and broken it.

Yet identifying the source of her alarm did nothing to stop her hands from shaking or to dispel the dizziness that swept over her. Gripping the wheel, she eased back on the gas pedal, willing herself to focus on the road as she traversed the short distance to Sam's street.

When she made the final turn and the house he'd described came into view, however, the shaking became so severe that she was forced to pull to the side of the road or risk losing control. She sensed danger here as surely as she'd sensed it that night at the restaurant parking lot, when a prickle at the base of her spine had alerted her to trouble—seconds too late.

Well, it wasn't too late now. She could still turn around. Go back to Philly.

But that would put her no closer to a solution to her problem than she'd been before, she acknowledged. Short of seeking professional counseling, this was the only option that seemed to offer even a remote chance of jump-starting her recovery. If things didn't work out, she could always try therapy. But she'd disappoint both herself and Liz if she didn't give this a chance.

As she struggled to get her breathing under control, Cara studied the modest bungalow that Sam now called home. In contrast to the condo they'd shared in the fashionable Society Hill area of Philadelphia, the house was simple and unpretentious. Constructed of redbrick and stone, with a generous front porch, it looked to date from the forties or fifties. Stately oak trees in the large yard sheltered the dwelling, and a climbing rosebush covered with profuse pink blossoms cascaded over a white lattice arbor on the side.

It looked homey, Cara reflected. The kind of place that would welcome you back after a long day. And it looked safe, just as Sam had promised. More than anything, that appealed to Cara. If she could feel secure here, maybe this would be the answer to her prayers after all.

Putting her trust in the Lord, Cara shifted the car back into gear and moved forward.

Not until the car started to roll again did Sam exhale.

He'd been standing at the edge of the large picture window in his living room for the past fifteen minutes, watching for Cara. Her plane had landed on schedule— he'd checked. He'd calculated the approximate time it would take her to claim luggage and pick up her rental car. He knew the precise duration of the drive from the airport to Oak Hill. She was right on schedule.

When the unfamiliar car had stopped at the end of his street, however, he'd panicked. Assuming it was Cara, he'd been prepared to bolt from the house and run after her if she got cold feet and turned around.

Much to his relief, that hadn't happened.

Yet.

But it still could, he conceded. And if it did, he'd deal with it. In the meantime, he had other problems to worry about, the most pressing one being the worst case of nerves he'd had since the night he'd proposed.

Sam knew this was his last chance to repair the damage he'd inflicted on their marriage. He also knew he had to be prudent and careful in his approach. If Cara discovered his hidden agenda, she'd disappear as quickly as the deer he sometimes startled on the rural roads he often traversed. The operative words were patience, consideration and—most important of all, he reminded himself—communication. His weakness. He'd never been very good at expressing his feelings, but he was even willing to ask the Almighty for help in overcoming that impediment if that's what it took to win back his wife.

The car slowed to a stop in front of his house, and he watched as Cara opened the door and exited, as eager for his first glimpse of her as a sea-weary sailor is for the sight of land.

She stood beside the car for a few seconds, giving Sam a chance to savor her shoulder-length, springy red curls. Burnished by the late-afternoon sun, the color was as glorious and full of life as he remembered. Then she reached for her handbag, slung it over her shoulder and moved around the front of the car.

When she started up the curving stone walkway toward his front door, Sam shifted back a bit into the shadows and continued to scrutinize her. Black slacks hugged her trim hips, and her soft, black-and-white-striped knit top hinted at her curves. A smile whispered at the corners of his mouth as he recalled the way he used to tease her about being a slender chef, suggesting that a slim figure wasn't a good advertisement for her culinary skills. She'd always countered by saying that it demonstrated her remarkable discipline, yet never failed to lament that she could afford to lose a few pounds.

Well, she couldn't afford to anymore, he realized, his smile fading as the setting sun backlit her, emphasizing her too-willowy five-foot-six silhouette. She'd lost more than a few pounds since he'd last seen her. Too many, in fact. And as she drew closer, he saw other indications of the toll the stress had taken on her. Her face, though a bit pale, was as beautiful as always, the smooth forehead, pert nose, soft, full lips, and strong, determined chin just as he remembered. And her startling green eyes were still fringed by those amazing long lashes. But the shadows beneath them, along with the tense line of her jaw and her taut lips, provided clear evidence of the lingering effects of her recent trauma.

Thanks to Oak Hill's sheriff, Dale Lewis, Sam now had a better handle on the incident that had triggered Cara's visit. After years on the police force in L.A., Dale had law enforcement contacts all over the country—including Philly. At Sam's request, he'd been able to get a police report on the incident and recap it for Sam.

According to the investigating officer's write-up, Cara and her coworker, Tony, had been the last to leave the restaurant that night. As they crossed the parking lot, a masked gunman had accosted them, demanding their money. While Cara had handed over her purse at once, Tony had balked. As a result, the perpetrator had grabbed Cara, put the gun to her head and told Tony to toss his wallet on the ground or she'd be history. Tony had complied, but as the robber pushed Cara aside and reached for the wallet, Tony had lunged at him. The man had shot Tony, then run off.

A passerby heard the gunfire and called the police, but by the time they arrived Tony was dead. No suspects had yet been arrested. Cara had been questioned but could remember few details of the shooting, and the assailant's mask prevented her from making an ID. However, with her purse in hand, he could identify *her*.

Dale's summary had left Sam with a sick feeling in the pit of his stomach. If the gunman had been high, or desperate for a fix, or worried about witnesses despite his mask, he could have shot Cara, too. Killed her. The very possibility caused Sam's blood to run cold. And strengthened his resolve to do whatever it took to let her know how much he cherished her, and how sorry he was for the mess he'd made of things.

As Cara stepped up to the door, Sam rubbed his hands down his jeans. Even before the highest-stake surgeries, he'd never gotten sweaty palms. He'd been sure of his ability to save lives. But he wasn't anywhere near as confident in his relationship skills as he was wielding a scalpel. Especially when his future was on the line.

Moving to the door, Sam took a steadying breath and pulled it wide, forcing his stiff lips to curve into the semblance of a smile. "Hello, Cara. Welcome."

Her finger poised to ring the bell, Cara froze.

When the silence lengthened, Sam spoke again. "I'm glad you made it safe and sound. Come in." He stepped aside.

"I left my things in the car, and I didn't lock it." She cast an uncertain look over her shoulder.

"They'll be fine. You're not in Philly anymore. I'll get them in a few minutes." Though she appeared unconvinced, she stepped over the threshold. "Did you have any problem finding your way?"

"No. You were always good at giving directions."

But not other things. Sam almost voiced that thought, then restrained the impulse. It was too soon to get so personal. "Would you like something to drink?"

"No. I'd prefer to get settled in and unpack."

"Of course. You've had a long day." He'd worried how she would cope with the stresses of the trip, but aside from her slight pallor, she seemed okay. "Let me show you around, then I'll get your things."

He gave her a quick tour of the house—the sunny kitchen with attached breakfast room that overlooked a private backyard; the back porch, inviting but bare; an empty dining room; an underfurnished living room featuring a lone couch in front of the fireplace with a table, lamp and straight chair beside it; his uncluttered office. He identified a closed door as his bedroom when they passed, but didn't pause until they reached the last room at the end of the hall. Stepping aside, he ushered her in. "I hope this will be okay."

Based on the sparse furnishings in the rest of the house, Cara wasn't expecting much. Certainly nothing like the exquisite room waiting for her when she stepped over the threshold.

The walls were washed in her favorite shade of aquamarine, the smell of fresh paint still in the air. A queen-size brass bed sported an ivory dust ruffle and a comforter in a Monet-like print in shades of blue, green and lavender. A matching valance hung over the large window. There was an overstuffed chair, a reading lamp, a small TV and an antique walnut dresser with a large oval mirror above it. A cut-crystal vase of old-fashioned pink roses graced the nightstand, their fragrance wafting through the room.

"There's a private bath, too." Sam followed her in and swung open a door to reveal a spacious, modern bath replete with granite countertops and fluffy towels.

Stunned, Cara could only gape at the lovely suite she knew he'd prepared just for her.

"If there's anything else you need, I hope you'll feel free to let me know."

After living with Sam for ten years, Cara was familiar with every nuance of his voice. She heard the uncertainty now, sensed his tension and trepidation. This couldn't be easy for him, either, she realized, whatever his motives might be. There was too much history between them to allow a comfortable co-existence. At the very least her presence would disrupt his life, alter his routine. Yet he'd gone out of his way to make her feel welcome.

She looked around again, troubled by something about the arrangement. Then it hit her. Considering the attached bath, this had to be the master suite.

Frowning, she turned to him. "Was this your room?"

A dismissive shrug preceded his words. "It was more space than I needed."

"I can't take your room."

"It's done, Cara. These aren't my colors. I'm more an earth-tones kind of guy." A grin tugged at one corner of his mouth. "Just enjoy it."

At his unexpected generosity, her throat tightened with an emotion so long absent from her life that it took her a moment to identify it.

Tenderness.

And that wasn't good. Sam could be charming; he'd demonstrated that early in their relationship. But she knew about his other qualities, too. The self-absorbed preoccupation that had changed into bitterness after his life was turned upside down, and an anger so cold and hard, so close to violence, that it had frightened her and made living with him stressful and difficult. It would be wise to remember those aspects of his personality if she found her attitude toward him beginning to soften.

"I appreciate all you did. I didn't expect you to go to any trouble on my behalf." Her voice sounded stiff even to her own ears. But if Sam noticed her sudden aloofness, he let it pass.

"It was no trouble. I'll get your bags."

Before she had a chance to regroup, he was back, her carry-on and larger suitcase in tow. "Shall I leave these by the closet?" he asked.

"Yes. Thanks."

Setting them down, he turned to her. "When I did rounds at the medical center in Rolla earlier I picked up some Chinese food for tonight. I hope that's okay. Oak Hill has many attributes, but fine dining isn't among them. There's a Middle Eastern restaurant, but the food's a bit spicy for my taste. And of course, there's Gus's. Okay for a turkey sandwich now and then, but I wouldn't recommend it for much more. He only knows one way to cook—deep fried." Once more, the whisper of a smile teased his lips.

"Chinese sounds good. Thank you. But I can take care of my own meals after today."

"However you want to arrange things is fine with me, Cara."

His gentle response to her defensive comment made her feel like an ingrate. She tried again. "It's just that I don't want to upset your routine any more than necessary. It might be easier if we each do our own thing."

"Sure." He headed back to the door, pausing on the threshold. "I'll be in my office. Let me know when you'd like dinner. I'm in no hurry if you want to take a shower or a quick nap first."

Without waiting for a reply, he turned and closed the door behind him.

For several minutes, Cara stood unmoving, overwhelmed by Sam's efforts to welcome her—and more than a little nervous about his motives. He'd gone way above and beyond simple hospitality. You didn't vacate, redecorate and furnish a master suite for a mere guest. When she'd agreed to come, all she'd been looking for was a simple room in a safe place where she could begin to put the nightmare of the murder behind her. She didn't need—or want—any complications. And she'd been clear about that with Sam. He knew where she stood. If he was expecting anything more, that was his problem.

Suddenly weary, Cara slipped off her shoes and sat on the bed, tempted by Sam's suggestion of a quick nap. It was amazing how the mere presence of another human being could provide the elusive peace of mind that had kept her awake through the long, dark, endless nights since the attack. If Sam offered her nothing else during this visit, that would be enough.

Scooting onto the bed, she stretched out and closed her eyes. She'd give herself twenty minutes, she decided. Then she'd be ready for dinner.

Sam stood outside Cara's door, debating his next move. Three hours had passed. Dusk had descended, and the rumbles in his stomach were growing more persistent. While the hectic schedule in his old life had often dictated late dinners, since moving to Oak Hill he'd become accustomed to a six o'clock evening meal. He'd missed that by two and a half hours.

But he was far more worried about Cara than his protesting stomach. He'd stopped outside her door a couple of times, but he'd never heard a sound. No running water, no drawers being opened and closed, no muted background noise to suggest she'd turned on the TV.

Acutely aware that she wanted her space, he was loath to invade it already. But he was beginning to think that she might be ill. Earlier, he'd attributed her paleness to fatigue and stress from the trip. Perhaps he'd been wrong. Yet if she was sick, if she needed anything, he suspected that asking him for help would be the last option she'd pursue. She'd push him away, much as he'd pushed her away when he'd most needed help.

Torn, Sam wavered, realizing even as he vacillated how much he'd changed in the past couple of years. He'd once been decisive. Confident he had all the answers. In control. That sense of self-importance—of omnipotence, almost—had been honed by his professional success, he now realized. And it had spilled over into his personal life—to the detriment of his marriage. If nothing else, the violence that had been directed against him had destroyed that arrogance. The reining in of his ego might be the one good thing that had resulted from the nightmare, he reflected.

Making a decision at last, Sam reached up. But as he stood poised to knock, he paused to stare at the scars on the back of his hand. From just above his wrist to the tips of his fingers, there wasn't a square inch untouched by the network of shiny white lines. Even now, almost two years after the attack, his hand remained slightly mis-shapen, the function improved but still impaired. Though he maintained the physical therapy regime prescribed by his doctors, and continued to note small improvements, his fingers would never regain the dexterity required to perform surgery. Bill West had achieved his goal.

A flash of terror from that dark night, along with a rec-ollection of acute pain, swept over Sam. While he hadn't been able to control the nightmares that had plagued him in the beginning, it had been months since he'd let himself think about the incident that had robbed him of his career.

And this wasn't the time to start. He'd moved past that, gone on with his life. Thanks to the skill of the col-leagues who had reconstructed his hand with painstak-ing care, he'd recovered far more function than anyone had dared hope for. Considering that his hand had been smashed beyond recognition, and factoring in the exten-sive nerve damage he'd suffered, the fact that he could use it at all was nothing short of a miracle—if one believed in such things.

Putting such reflections aside, Sam forced himself to knock on the door. Cara might not be pleased at the in-trusion. But too often in his marriage he'd held back, pulled away and shut the window to his heart at the very time he should have thrown wide the door and invited her in. Only in retrospect had Sam recognized how hurtful that had been to his wife—and how damaging it had been to their relationship. He wasn't going to make that mistake again. This time, he was going to follow his heart.

No matter the risk that entailed.

Chapter Four

A faint rapping penetrated Cara's consciousness, tugging her back from a deep slumber she didn't want to relinquish. Not when it was the most restful sleep she'd enjoyed in weeks. Turning on her side, she buried her head in the down pillow, drifting off in a matter of seconds when the room grew silent.

Unfortunately, the quiet didn't last long. The rapping started again, more insistent this time. And too loud to ignore. But it was the muffled question, the words laced with apprehension, that pulled her back to reality.

"Cara? Are you okay?"

Struggling to shake off the heavy sleep, Cara opened her eyes. The dim room, illuminated only by the glow of a light somewhere beyond the large, unshuttered window, wasn't familiar. But the voice was.

"Cara, please answer me!"

Where was she? And what was Sam doing here?

The dots still weren't connecting in her sleep-fuzzy brain. With a triumph of mind over body, she forced her lethargic arms to respond and tried to push herself into a sitting position, hoping the fog would clear once she was upright.

Just as she managed to get vertical, the door cracked open. And as light from the hall spilled across the bottom of the bed, spotlighting the Monet-patterned comforter, the pieces fell into place. She was in Oak Hill. At Sam's house. She'd lain down to take a twenty-minute nap.

Except that didn't make sense, she realized, turning toward the window. It had been bright daylight when she'd stretched out. Now it was dusk.

"Sorry to intrude, but I've been knocking for a while. I wanted to make sure you were okay."

At the sound of Sam's voice, she turned back. He was little more than a silhouette, his face unreadable in the shadows. Shoving her hair back, she peered at her watch in the dim light. "What time is it?"

"Eight-thirty."

"You're kidding!"

"No. Is it all right if I turn on a light?"

"Sure."

He felt along the wall, then flicked on the switch. The lamp on the dresser came on, bathing the room in a mellow glow.

Blinking, Cara tried to rub the sleep out of her eyes. "I'm sorry. I don't know what happened. I only planned to take a quick nap. And I can't imagine why I didn't hear your knock." She slept so lightly these days that the slightest sound brought her instantly awake—and alert.

"When did you last have a block of uninterrupted sleep?"

"I don't know." More to the point, when had she last felt *safe* enough to indulge in a block of uninterrupted sleep?

"Considering what you went through, that's not unusual. Stress can cause insomnia, and that, in turn, often leads to more stress. It can become a vicious cycle that results in a serious anxiety disorder." He waited, as if giving her a chance to comment. To her relief, he didn't push when she ignored the overture. "In any case, let's hope you can break that cycle while you're here. I think you made a good start tonight. Are you hungry?"

She was surprised to discover that she was. Her appetite had been another casualty of the trauma. "Yes. Give me a minute."

"I'll meet you in the kitchen." He closed the door behind him.

In view of the late hour, she did no more than run a brush through her hair and touch up her lipstick. Nevertheless, by the time she joined him he'd already put plates and utensils on the oak table. When she paused in the doorway, he was removing a steaming plate of chicken and broccoli from the microwave.

He looked good, she thought, taking a moment to observe him before he noticed her. Sam hadn't often worn jeans in Philadelphia, but she'd always liked the way they emphasized his long, lean legs. And his blue knit sport shirt not only matched his eyes, it accentuated the width of his shoulders and his broad chest. There were more glints of silver than she remembered in his short, sandy hair. But that just gave him a distinguished air. The cobalt blue of his eyes hadn't changed, though the fine lines around them were new. As were the faint grooves at the corners of his mouth. It seemed the past thirteen months hadn't been easy on him, either.

A smile warmed his face when he spotted her. "That was fast." He set the plate next to a bowl of rice. "What would you like to drink?"

"Water will be fine." He was still wearing his wedding ring, she realized, her gaze riveted to his hand. Just as she was. Somehow, she hadn't expected that.

Returning to the counter, he slid a plate of what looked like Mongolian beef into the microwave, closed the door and punched some buttons. Then he retrieved a glass from the cabinet. "This will be ready in a couple of minutes. Have a seat."

"I hope I didn't delay your dinner too long." She slid into her chair.

"Not a problem."

"You always were a late eater." She thought about the days when it hadn't been uncommon for him to wolf down dinner at nine or ten o'clock at night, then head for his study to do a couple more hours of paperwork before turning in.

"Not anymore." He deposited her glass on the table.

Surprised, she angled a look up at him. "Why not?"

"I ate late in those days because that was the only time I could fit it in. The pace here is quite a bit slower. Oak Hill isn't Philly, and family practice isn't surgery. Go ahead and help yourself."

Cara watched as he retrieved the beef from the microwave and joined her at the table. His new life sounded quite a bit different from his old one, and she was curious about it. But if she wanted to keep things simple, it was best to avoid personal topics.

As he reached for the bowl of rice, Cara bowed her head. He paused, waiting until she finished her silent prayer of thanks before filling his plate.

"I'm surprised you continue to find comfort in that after all that's happened," he remarked.

Hearing none of the expected sarcasm, she gave him an honest reply. "Now more than ever."

At her quiet response, he sent her a questioning look but remained silent.

"I take it you never got into the habit?" She scooped out some rice.

"I'm even less inclined now…after all that's happened."

"Times of trauma are often when we need Him the most," Cara suggested, keeping her tone conversational as she dipped into the Mongolian beef.

"Maybe."

Given his noncommittal reply, Cara decided a change of subject was in order. They never had meshed in their views of faith, and there was no reason to suppose they'd start now. In the beginning of their marriage, Sam had gone to church with Cara because he'd recognized the important role it played in her life. But it had never had the same meaning for him. And as their relationship faltered, she'd found herself attending church alone more and more often. Though it saddened her that he'd never connected with the Lord, his life was no longer her concern. She needed to remember that.

"Why don't you tell me how you've positioned my visit to your friends here, so we can be sure our stories are straight." She was curious to hear his answer in light of the fact that he was still wearing his ring.

Sam thought about her question. He didn't have any friends in Oak Hill, not in the way she meant. Just patients and a few acquaintances. "I said you'd taken a leave after going far too long without a vacation, and that you needed a quiet place to relax and unwind," he replied, choosing his words with care. "I mentioned that we're separated but friendly. I know that's stretching the truth a bit, but short of getting into a lot of history I doubt either of us wants to dredge up, that was the easiest way to explain it."

"That works for me."

Relieved, he ladled a spoonful of the chicken and broccoli onto his plate. "What did you tell your family?"

"That I'd be out of town for a bit. Everyone has my cell number, and that's how they always call me. Besides, Mom and Dad are in Africa for a year on a mission trip, so all our communication is by e-mail anyway."

"Liz mentioned that."

Tilting her head, Cara looked at him, wondering what else Liz had told him. "Did she fill you in on Bev?"

"She just said your sister and her family are getting ready to move. And that Bev is pregnant. It was pretty clear that spending time with your family wasn't an option."

"No, it wasn't. Besides, I didn't see any reason to worry them with my problems. They all have enough on their minds as it is. What about your mom? What did you tell her?"

"Nothing. I always call her from the office. Every Friday morning, before the weekly bridge game she hosts. That's about the only time I'm sure to connect with her. Since my aunt became a widow and they both moved into that retirement community in California, their social schedule is something to behold."

A smile tugged at Cara's mouth. She'd always liked Sam's mother. Quiet, unassuming, introspective and brilliant—she was very much like her only child. It was nice to hear that she was cutting loose and enjoying an active social life in her golden years. Maybe Sam could learn a few more lessons from her, she mused.

"I'm glad your mom is enjoying herself. And it sounds like we're covered." Relieved, she reached for her glass of water.

"Until the locals start asking questions."

Her hand froze and she shot him a startled look.

The hint of a smile teased his lips. "This is a small town, Cara. People talk. And there's a very active grapevine. Almost as good as the *Gazette*—our local paper— when it comes to spreading news. Although I've laid the groundwork, you can expect to get a few discreet but leading questions."

"That shouldn't be a problem." She set the glass back down. "I don't plan to mingle much, anyway."

Liz's comment about Cara holing up in her apartment since the attack echoed in his mind. Considering that his wife had always been a social person, isolation couldn't be healthy. "I don't mean to give you the wrong impression. It's a very nice town, and the people are genuine and caring. It might be fun to explore a bit. I guarantee you can't get lost."

Cara shrugged. "I'll see. I brought along quite a few books, and I expect that will occupy most of my days."

"Whatever you want, Cara." Better to back off than turn her off, he decided. "This is your time."

For the rest of the meal, Sam did his best to make small talk. But he'd never been very adept at it. Even in the good times of their marriage he'd been content to let Cara carry the bulk of the conversational burden. And that's what it had always been to him— a burden. Cara, on the other hand, had been a master at drawing people out. For her, it was as natural as breathing.

Yet tonight their positions were reversed. She was subdued and reticent, giving brief answers, content to listen in silence as he told her about the town and some of the personalities. Yet another example of the profound effect the trauma had had on her, he realized. Her normal response would have been to pepper him with questions, her eyes alight with interest. Instead, she kept her gaze downcast, focused on her food, and responded only when asked a direct question. Though her body bore physical signs of her stress, it was her personality shift that most alarmed Sam. He was beginning to better understand—and appreciate—Liz's concern.

When they finished the meal and he insisted on taking care of the dishes, Cara didn't argue, as she once would have. Instead, she quietly thanked him and disappeared down the hall.

As Sam watched her go, he hoped that the Lord had listened to the earlier prayer of His wayward son. Because reaching the woman he loved was beginning to look like a far more difficult challenge than he'd even imagined. And he could sure use the extra help.

* * *

For the second time in a dozen hours, an intermittent, muffled noise penetrated Cara's deep slumber.

Despite her three-hour nap, she'd once again drifted off to sleep with a speed that astounded her after her late dinner with Sam. And she knew why. She might not trust her heart to the man she'd married, but she felt safe in his presence. And that feeling of safety had chased away the fears that had kept her awake—and anxious—through the long nights she'd spent alone since the attack.

The sleep felt so good, so renewing, that she didn't want to wake up. Yet there was something familiar about the sound that tugged her back to consciousness.

Staring up at the dark ceiling, she listened. But soon the house grew silent again. Could she have imagined the noise? Had it been some scrap of elusive dream deep in her subconscious?

When the silence lengthened, her eyelids once more grew heavy. Whatever it was, she wasn't going to worry about it. Sam was a few steps down the hall. If there was anything to be concerned about, he'd deal with it. It was his house, after all.

As she began to fall back sleep, however, the noise started again. Louder now.

Alarmed, Cara sat up and scooted to the edge of the bed, adrenaline surging through her. Her hands shaking, she fumbled in the dark for the small canister of mace that hadn't been more than an arm's length away any night since the murder. Clutching it in trembling fingers, she rose and moved to her door, cracking it the tiniest bit.

The corridor, illuminated by the dim glow of a night-light, was empty. But the sounds were louder. And they were coming from Sam's room.

Now Cara knew why the noise had seemed familiar. She'd heard it often. After Sam had been released from the hospital, nightmares had often plagued him. He'd thrashed about with such force that Cara had limped for a week when he'd once kicked her in the calf in his sleep. After that he'd insisted on moving to the guest room. And he'd never returned.

But even then, she'd gone to him during the night whenever his agonized cries had awakened her, wanting to hold him, to comfort him, to let him know that she cared. Though he'd pushed her away, she'd kept trying. Until he'd lashed out once too often in bitterness and venomous anger, telling her that she couldn't do anything to help him—that no one could—and she'd finally believed him. After that, she'd listened night after night, helpless to do anything more than pray, as he battled his demons alone.

The same ones he seemed to be battling still.

As she crept down the hall, stopping outside his door, Cara's throat tightened with emotion. The fact that he continued to suffer from nightmares almost two years after the incident that had triggered them underscored the depth of his trauma. Her experience had been horrifying, true. But it hadn't been a personal vendetta, carried out with calculating ruthlessness. Nor had it robbed her of the work she loved, changing her life forever.

The thrashing intensified and, fearing Sam would injure himself, she gave a sharp rap on the door.

"Sam? Sam, wake up!" When the thrashing persisted, along with the familiar cries that had always torn at her heart, she knocked louder and raised her volume. It always took a lot to wake him from these dreams. "Sam! Wake up, Sam!"

She kept at it, until all at once the sounds stopped and the house grew quiet. She waited, but when the silence continued, she spoke again—with less certainty. "Sam? Are you all right?"

"Yes. I'm sorry I woke you." The words came out hoarse and ragged.

"Can I…do you need anything?" She hadn't planned to make that offer. But no matter her feelings about Sam, it went against her nature to turn away from anyone in need without attempting to help.

"No. I'm sorry for disturbing you. Go back to bed."

Glancing at her watch, Cara noted the time. Three o'clock. A long way until morning, she realized with a sigh. And she had a feeling she wasn't going to fall back to sleep with anywhere near the same ease she'd drifted off earlier in the evening.

On the other side of the door, Sam struggled to regain control. Forcing himself to take deep, even breaths, he managed to slow his pulse and respiration. But he couldn't stop the tremors that racked his body.

What in the world was going on? It had been weeks since he'd had the nightmare that had plagued him for months after the attack. A dream so terrifying, so real, that he'd fought off sleep each night as long as he could. Yet time hadn't diminished its horror.

Tonight, once again, he'd relived that late return to the parking garage below the condo. Felt the prickle of unease race along his spine as he'd left his car, sensing some ominous presence. Tasted fear as the dark-clothed figure emerged from the shadows, just out of sight of the security cameras, a gun pointed in his direction.

As his temples began to throb—another familiar consequence of the dream—Sam pulled himself upright in the bed. Drawing his legs up, he rested his elbows on his knees and cradled his pounding head in his hands. He tried to stem the tide of memories, tried to bury them, but it was impossible after the nightmare. They were too fresh, too vivid. The attack was as real as if it had happened yesterday. As were the incidents leading up to it.

In retrospect, Sam knew he hadn't been in top form going into surgery on the fateful day that had set the tragic events in motion. But he'd attributed his slight nausea to a simple upset stomach. Though he could have asked a colleague to take over for him, he'd been convinced that no one could do the operation better than him—even if he wasn't a hundred percent. Another example of his arrogance in those days.

But then things had started to go wrong. As the surgery progressed, and the simple upset stomach evolved into an acute pain, he'd begun to fumble. Make mistakes. When he'd finally acknowledged that he was too ill to continue, a colleague had to be rushed in to complete the job.

Sam had recovered from the surgery prompted by his appendicitis attack. But his patient—Claire West—had died. Consumed by anger and grief, the woman's husband had demanded an investigation.

After Sam was cleared of any wrongdoing, everyone had thought that was the end of it. Until the night Bill West, his reasoning clouded by grief and anger, had confronted Sam in the condo's basement parking garage. After forcing Sam into the shadows at gunpoint, then motioning for him to turn around, he'd spoken. Barely more than a dozen words. But they were forever etched in Sam's brain.

"I can't bring Claire back. But I'm going to make sure you never kill anyone again."

Sam had assumed the man meant to shoot him. An assumption that seemed borne out when a sharp pain had ricocheted through his head, and the world had gone black.

As it turned out, though, Bill West had had another kind of punishment in store for his wife's surgeon.

When Sam awakened, lying on the floor of the garage, he'd been aware of two things. A relentless throbbing in his head—and an excruciating pain in his right hand. He'd tried to move his fingers, but they hadn't responded. When his vision cleared and he could finally shift his head enough to look toward his hand, the reason had become clear. Swollen and misshapen, his hand had been smashed almost beyond recognition. Through the haze of pain, he knew that multiple bones had been broken, and he suspected the man had inflicted extensive nerve damage as well.

Somehow he'd extracted his cell phone and called 911. And he'd managed to remain conscious long enough to identify the perpetrator for the police. Later he'd learned that they'd discovered the man at his home, a short note beside his body: "I did what I had to do. May Claire rest in peace."

Through all of the pain and bitterness and despair that had followed, Sam had tried to hate the man who'd destroyed his life. Yet part of him feared the man's accusation had merit. Sam had made mistakes in the operating room that day. He knew that, as did his team. However, he hadn't considered any of them serious enough to contribute to the woman's death. Neither had the review board. But he couldn't help wondering if he was at fault. If Claire West—and her husband—were dead because of him. That burden continued to weigh him down, and he was still trying to find a way to deal with the guilt.

For the most part, he'd managed to confine the battle to daylight hours.

Until tonight.

Cara's arrival couldn't be coincidental, he realized. She'd stood by him through the whole ordeal, despite the fact that he'd given her nothing but abuse. Angry at the world, he'd lashed out at the closest available target. Meeting her encouragement with sarcasm, her suggestions of prayer with ridicule, her gestures of love with indifference, he'd driven her away bit by bit. And even when the nightmares began to recede, when his hand had begun to heal and they could once more have safely shared a bed, they remained in separate rooms by unspoken mutual consent.

It was then that Sam realized how much he missed her. How much he needed her. But just as his awkward hand no longer seemed to know how to touch an object without breaking it, neither did his heart know how to reach out and touch the woman he loved without hurting her more.

In time, his desperate loneliness had driven him to a local bar. Alcohol hadn't helped much, but Amber's interest had. The blond waitress had given the bar's newest customer more than his fair share of attention. And that had led to the night he'd driven the final wedge in his marriage, splitting it in two.

Lifting his head, Sam stared into the darkness of his bedroom, his expression bleak. How could he ever hope to win Cara back after the way he'd treated her? Yet how could he go on if he didn't? All these months, as he'd tried to build a new life for himself, the one thing that had kept him going was the hope that he would find a way to convince Cara to give their marriage another try. But now, despite her presence in his home, the obstacles seemed insurmountable.

And he wasn't in any condition to deal with them tonight, he realized, as the throbbing in his head intensified. He needed aspirin. Several. Quickly.

Swinging his feet to the floor, he stood, bracing himself with one hand against the wall. When his legs steadied, he covered the short distance to the door, pulled it open—and stopped short.

Cara was still standing in the hall, dressed in one of those sleep shirts she'd always favored, a can of mace clutched in one hand, reminding him yet again that he wasn't the only who lived with trauma. She gasped and took a step back at his sudden appearance.

"Cara…I'm sorry." He reached out a hand, imploring, then let it drop to his side. "I thought you'd gone back to bed." A shiver rippled through him, and he realized that his T-shirt was drenched with sweat.

"Headache?" Cara's question came out in an unsteady whisper and her features softened in compassion.

"Yeah. Aspirin will take care of it. Look, I'm sorry about this. It hasn't happened in weeks. This won't be a habit." Even as he made the promise, he hoped it was one he could keep.

As if sensing his thoughts, she spoke, her tone subdued. "Nightmares aren't easy to control."

Sam knew from Liz that Cara was speaking from personal experience. And he'd been prepared to comfort her if necessary, as she had once comforted him. Instead, he'd been the one plagued by bad dreams while she slept soundly.

The irony wasn't lost on him.

"I'll do my best," he responded.

Half-turning, she hesitated and looked over her shoulder. "Do you want me to get the aspirin for you?"

The trepidation in her eyes, the uncertainty, reminded him of the countless occasions when he'd snarled out an ungrateful response to such an offer. And filled him with gratitude that she'd been willing to risk reaching out once again.

Gentling his voice, he did his best to summon up a smile. "Thank you, but I can manage. You need your sleep. I'll be okay by morning. Good night."

Without waiting for a reply, he headed for the bathroom. Once there, he steadied himself on the edge of the sink, filled a glass with water and downed several aspirin in one gulp. Sitting on the edge of the tub, he drew steadying breaths until he felt able to make the trip back to his room.

When he stepped into the hall, the corridor was deserted. Yet glancing toward Cara's room, he noted that the door was cracked a fraction of an inch. Had she forgotten to close it? Or had she left it that way on purpose, so she could hear if Sam had any further problems?

Sam assumed it was the former. She was tired, and it was the middle of the night, after all. No one thought clearly at this hour.

But for tonight, anyway, he was going to pretend it was the latter. Because if he allowed himself to believe she cared, he suspected that fantasy would do more than anything else to keep further nightmares at bay.

Chapter Five

"Hi. You must be Cara. I'm Marge Sullivan. Welcome to Oak Hill. Glad to see you arrived safe and sound yesterday."

Juggling a mug of coffee in one hand, Cara stared at the vision standing on the other side of Sam's front door. Well past middle-age, her gray hair cut in a trendy, spiky style, the woman wore lime-green capri pants and a gauzy, green-and-orange print tunic top nipped in at her stout waist with a gold chain-link belt.

When the unexpected visitor thrust out her hand, Cara was left with no choice but to take it. "Yes, I'm Cara. Thank you for the welcome."

"Oh, we're real neighborly around here." The woman gave Cara's hand a vigorous pump before releasing it. "I was in to see Dr. Martin last week. Hurt my knee a few years back, and every now and then it decides to cause a little trouble. Guess I'm just getting old." She paused long enough to let loose with a hearty chuckle. "Anyway, he mentioned you were coming and I thought it might be nice to bring a little welcome gift." She held out a plastic-wrapped package of what appeared to be homemade cinnamon rolls. "I know I probably shouldn't be giving food to a chef. But these are our specialty at the Oak Hill Inn. Seemed like the best thing to bring."

"Thank you. This is very kind." Cara accepted the rolls, feeling at a loss. During dinner last night, Sam had given her a rundown on the town, as well as some of the residents, and she had a vague recollection of someone named Marge. But she'd been so busy trying to come to grips with the bizarre scenario of dining with her estranged husband in his home that she hadn't paid much attention. A lapse she now regretted.

"The Oak Hill Inn is…the B and B?"

"Yes. A giant Victorian monstrosity I inherited from an aunt. Nice, if you like that sort of thing. I don't. But the guests seem to. They think it's romantic. I've had more than a few couples tell me a weekend in the Rose Room has put a spark back into their marriage."

Uncomfortable with that remark, Cara decided to change the subject. "I must say, your timing was perfect. I was getting ready to have breakfast when you rang the bell. These will be a real treat, Ms. Sullivan."

"Call me Marge. I hope the room Dr. Martin was fixing up for you turned out okay. I offered to help, but he said he had it under control."

Casting another discreet glance over Marge's attire, Cara tried not to shudder. *Thank you, Lord.* "It's lovely. I'm sure I'll be very comfortable."

"Well, if I can help in any way during your visit, you be sure and let me know. I'm at the inn most of the time.

It's a couple blocks off Main Street, the other direction. Can't miss the place. Or I might be at church. And that reminds me. If you're looking for a place for Sunday worship, you'd be welcome to join us. It's the church with the big white steeple. You would have passed it on your way here yesterday. I'm sure you'd like our minister, Craig Andrews. He's a nice young man. Gives a good sermon, too."

"Thank you. I'll keep that in mind."

"I'm off, then. I've got a chamber of commerce board meeting downtown and I don't want to be late. Not that I have very far to travel." The woman chuckled again. "That's one of the nice things about living in a small town. Nothing's very far away. It will be quite a change for you after Philadelphia."

"Yes, I'm sure it will."

"Dr. Martin said you needed some time off and were looking for a nice, quiet place to rest. Take my word for it, you found the right spot. The most excitement we have around here is bingo at the American Legion Hall on Friday nights. And the annual ice-cream social in the fall. But I don't expect you'll be here for that."

"I don't think so."

"I wasn't real sure how long you planned to stay. Dr. Martin was a little vague about that."

When the woman paused, Cara realized she was expecting a response. Sam's comment that the townspeople were genuine and caring—but also curious—came back to her. As did his warning to expect a few discreet but leading questions. She figured Marge's last comment fit into that category, even if it wasn't technically a question.

"My plans are still up in the air." Cara smiled as she deflected the query, hoping the woman wouldn't take offense.

If Marge was put out by Cara's evasiveness, she didn't let on. "It's good to be flexible. We miss a lot of opportunities when we make up our minds about something and then put blinders on. Sometimes the forks in the road are the most interesting part of the journey. I know that was true for me when I left Boston and came here to take over the Oak Hill Inn." Checking her watch, she smiled at Cara. "Now I really will be late if I don't hustle. I baked those rolls first thing this morning, but they're cool by now. You might want to nuke 'em for a minute or two. They're a whole lot better warm. Take care now, and think about joining us at church."

With a wave, Marge turned and strode down the stone path, her gauzy top flapping in the morning breeze.

Feeling a bit overwhelmed, Cara closed the door and headed back to the kitchen. As she set the rolls on the counter, she reread the note Sam had propped against the toaster.

Cara: I'm sorry again about last night. I hope you were able to get back to sleep. You'll find eggs and English muffins in the fridge. Plus some deli things for lunch. Make yourself at home. See you tonight.

Picking up the slip of paper, Cara studied the scrawled words. Once, Sam had written in bold, precise strokes. She'd teased him about his penmanship on occasion, quipping that she was surprised he'd been admitted to medical school with such legible handwriting. But the attack had taken care of that. While he'd regained some flexibility, and had learned to compensate for his disability, it was clear he still had trouble wielding a pen. Another constant reminder of his trauma, one he would carry with him for the rest of his life.

As for going back to sleep last night…after the episode in the hall, it had taken her almost an hour to drift off. And when she'd finally awakened, Sam had been gone. But he'd left a set of house keys on the counter, along with a pot of coffee.

Pouring herself another cup of the strong brew, Cara peeled back the plastic wrap from Marge's offering, put one of the gooey rolls on a plate and slid it into the microwave. Within seconds the comforting aroma of cinnamon enveloped her. Marge's gesture had been kind, she acknowledged. And the woman had seemed friendly and sincere. Her attire might be a bit…flamboyant, but her candor and down-to-earth manner had been refreshing.

While Cara nibbled on the rich cinnamon roll, she poked around Sam's kitchen. The breakfast and lunch items he'd mentioned were front and center in his refrigerator, which was otherwise bare except for a quart of milk, butter, some single-serving packets of condiments and a few sodas.

What on earth did the man eat?

The freezer provided some answers. Microwave dinners were stacked in neat piles on the shelves. Farther down, she found a loaf of bread and a box of frozen waffles. A scan of the pantry revealed soup, cereal, crackers and tuna.

The cabinets yielded no additional food and only a meager supply of pots, pans and lids.

Dismayed, Cara topped off her mug. She supposed she should have expected an ill-equipped kitchen. Sam never had shown much interest in the culinary arts, preferring to spend his time on "important" things—an attitude that had manifested itself more and more as the years went on, causing additional strain on their marriage. Maybe she wasn't saving lives every day, but that didn't mean she wasn't adding enjoyment to life, enhancing special occasions, creating lasting memories. But he'd never seen it that way. And Cara had never been able to convince him that her career made a difference in people's lives, too.

Once more she surveyed the cabinets. Grateful as she was for the spectacular bedroom Sam had created for her, Cara knew she could never function in this kitchen. Nor could she exist on frozen commercial dinners. In the same way that surgery had given Sam a sense of self, cooking helped define Cara. Even after the shooting, when she'd been holed up in her apartment, she'd found refuge in her cooking, supplied with a steady stream of fresh ingredients by Liz. That had been the one normal thing in her life these past weeks. And she couldn't give it up.

Rummaging around in a drawer by the telephone, Cara found some scratch paper and a pen. Indulging herself with a second delectable cinnamon roll, she started compiling a list.

* * *

After retrieving his mail from the roadside box, Sam unlocked the front door, stepped inside—and stopped in his tracks.

Savory scents filled a house more accustomed to the unappetizing odor of burnt pizza than the mouthwatering smell of beef burgundy. And the delicious aromas wafting from the kitchen were far more appealing than the ones emanating from the bag in his hands, which contained whatever fried special Gus had featured tonight.

But Cara had been clear about the eating arrangements yesterday, he reminded himself. They were each to do their own thing. He'd agreed, and it was too late to renege. Besides, this visit was about giving her a place to stay where she felt safe and could rest. He shouldn't expect her to do anything for him—including cook.

Funny. In the old days, when Cara had always left a plate of something delicious for him to heat up after he returned home, he hadn't appreciated the blessing of the good food she'd lovingly prepared. But he'd had plenty of time to regret his lack of gratitude after they parted. Dinner was often a tasteless frozen entrée. Or worse, the indistinguishable meat and fish deep-fried by Gus, whose idea of flavoring was adding some cornmeal to his breading.

Closing the door behind him, Sam followed his nose to the kitchen door. In a rapid survey, he took in the unfamiliar pots, pans and bowls strewn about the counter. But it was Cara he focused on. Dressed in jeans and a T-shirt, a sturdy apron tied around her slender waist, she was occupied at the stove, a slight frown of concentration on her brow. She'd pulled back her curls with a barrette, revealing her delicate profile, and he drank in the sight of her. She looked good in his kitchen, he decided, propping a shoulder against the door frame as a tender smile teased the corners of his mouth.

"Looks like you've been busy."

Her hand jerked and she swung toward him, panic contorting her features. Sam straightened instantly, berating himself for his insensitivity. He should have warned her of his approach. "I'm sorry, Cara. I didn't mean to startle you."

Struggling to calm her racing pulse, Cara checked the clock on the wall by the table. Five-thirty. When Sam had said he finished work earlier now, she'd assumed he meant around seven o'clock. She'd expected to be done eating and cleaning up long before then.

"I—I didn't think you'd be home so soon." A tremor ran through her voice, and she cleared her throat, trying to erase the evidence of her fright.

"I close the office at five, unless there's an emergency. Look, I don't want to disturb you. I'll just grab a soda and let you finish up and enjoy your meal. I've got plenty of work to do in my study."

Her expression troubled, Cara watched as Sam extracted a can from the fridge, eyeing the white sack in his hand. It was clear he'd stopped somewhere for takeout. Since whatever he had in there smelled fried, she figured he'd paid a visit to Gus's.

"I didn't intend to oust you from your kitchen."

"This was always more your turf than mine, anyway. Where did you get all this stuff, by the way?" He waved a hand toward the stainless-steel pans, utensils, cutting board, and several things he couldn't identify.

"A shop in Rolla. Marge told me about it."

His eyebrows rose in surprise. She'd gone to Rolla. Alone. That seemed like a positive sign. Then again, considering his sparse kitchen, perhaps her trip had been more of an emergency run. But he decided not to comment, focusing instead on her reference to the local B and B owner.

"You met Marge?"

"Actually, she met me." A grin tugged at Cara's lips. "I found her at the door first thing this morning, cinnamon rolls in hand. Later, when I realized that your kitchen was…uh…a bit underequipped, I called the inn and asked her if she knew where I might buy a few things. I didn't realize she was the president of the chamber of commerce. She's a wealth of information."

"She is that." A matching grin softened Sam's mouth. "Leave me the bills for all this. I'll reimburse you. My kitchen needed furnishing anyway."

Shaking her head, she turned back to the stove. "Consider it a hostess gift. Or, in this case, a host gift. It's the least I can do. You may find them useful after I'm gone. And I'll make sure I'm not in your way tomorrow night."

He considered saying, *You're not in my way now, Cara*, then thought better of it. He had to be patient. Wait until she settled in, until she began to realize he had changed, before he launched his campaign to win her back. If he pushed too soon, she'd leave.

And he refused to even consider the "after I'm gone" part of her comment.

* * *

Two days later, the drone of a lawn mower somehow managed to penetrate the thick brick walls of Sam's air-conditioned house. The sound nudged Cara awake, reminding her of lazy summer days growing up in the suburbs of Cincinnati. The hum of a lawn mower had always been a pleasing sound to her. After living in apartments and condos for most her adult life, it had been years since she'd awakened to that comforting hum.

A peek at her watch confirmed that she'd slept later than usual. It was already eight forty-five. At this rate, she'd soon erase any lingering effects of sleep deprivation. In the three nights she'd spent in Sam's house, she figured she'd slept almost thirty hours. A piece of good news that she'd passed on to Liz when her friend had called yesterday, peppering her with questions.

"So how's it going with Sam?" Liz had asked at last, after they got past the nuts and bolts of Cara's trip and arrival. "Is it as awkward as you thought?"

"In some ways. We're like polite acquaintances, sort of tiptoeing around each other. But he's been good about giving me my space. The worst time is the evenings. I figured he'd be working late, but he gets home at a normal hour now. The first night, he got us Chinese. The second night, he disappeared with his take-out dinner to his study. Tonight, I ate early and went to my room so he wouldn't feel like he was a prisoner in his own house. We're still kind of playing it by ear."

"You'll work things out. And you sound much better already. I knew this was a good idea."

Refreshed from yet another sound night's sleep, Cara couldn't argue with her friend's conclusion. Swinging her feet to the plush carpet, she stood, stretched and wandered over to the window, lifting the shade a fraction to check the weather.

But the clear blue sky wasn't what she noticed when she glanced outside. Instead, her attention was riveted on the figure pushing the lawn mower at the back of the yard.

It was Sam.

Stunned, Cara could only stare. Sam had never, ever, shown any interest in yard work or manual labor. That was one of the reasons they'd bought a condo. The other was convenience. While Cara would have preferred a house in the suburbs, Sam had pointed out that the city location was more practical in light of their odd hours. She hadn't been able to argue with his logic.

Those considerations weren't important in Oak Hill, of course. It was no problem to have a house and yet live minutes from the business district. And condos no doubt were in short supply. That would explain why Sam had ended up with a house. But it didn't explain why he was cutting the grass. He could afford to hire someone to take care of unpleasant tasks like that if he wanted to. Which meant he hadn't wanted to. But why?

She had no idea.

And the answer to her next question was also elusive. Why was he home in the middle of the week?

Bewildered, Cara dressed and combed her hair, then added a touch of lipstick. Why she bothered with that, she wasn't sure. And she refused to consider the one obvious explanation—that Sam's presence led to her sudden decision to make herself a bit more presentable.

Wandering into the kitchen, Cara tried to focus on her English muffin and ignore the sight of Sam moving back and forth across the lawn. But her gaze kept wandering to the large window by the table until he disappeared around the side of the house.

She was sipping her second cup of coffee when the sound of a key being inserted into the back door alerted her to his imminent appearance. A few moments later he stepped into the house.

Surprise—and an emotion she was tempted to classify as pleasure—flashed across his face when he saw her at the table. "Good morning. Late breakfast?"

"I just got up."

He looked at her over his shoulder as he retrieved a mug and poured himself a cup of coffee. "I thought I heard you moving around about seven-thirty."

"I got up for a few minutes. But that comfortable bed called me back."

"Then I woke you."

"It was time I got up. And there aren't many more pleasant sounds to wake up to than a lawn mower."

He grinned. "Not many people would agree with that. My neighbors included."

"Too bad. Dad used to cut the grass on Saturday morning, and the sound always takes me back to a simpler time when things were predictable and ordinary and routine." Clearing her throat, Cara wrapped her fingers around her mug and stared into her coffee. *Too personal. Too revealing. Change the subject.* "Anyway, he always enjoyed doing it. But I didn't think you did."

"Things change, Cara. It feels good to be out in the sunshine. And I've discovered I like the smell of new-mown grass."

Unsure how to respond, Cara switched subjects. "I'm surprised you're home in the middle of the week."

Leaning back against the counter, he crossed one ankle over the other and took a sip of his coffee. "Isn't Wednesday the standard day off for doctors?"

"Yes. For most doctors. Not for you." Cara couldn't remember Sam taking a weekend or holiday off in years, let alone a Wednesday.

"I figured it was about time I got with the program."

Stymied once more, Cara remained silent.

"Besides, I don't always take the whole day off. If I have a patient at the medical center in Rolla, I visit them. And I volunteer for a few hours in the afternoon at a free rural clinic. You're welcome to come along if you're getting cabin fever. It's a pleasant drive, and there's a great antique store nearby. Not to mention a small park with benches. It would be a nice spot for reading."

Surprised by the offer, Cara started to decline—then hesitated. "Will you be back by dark?"

Taking another sip of coffee, Sam studied Cara. The sudden worry in her eyes told him that she was far from being over her fear of staying alone in the dark. She might be sleeping better, but she had a long way to go before she put the trauma behind her. "Yes. I'm always back by five. Some days a lot sooner."

Relief eased the tension in her features. "I think I'll

stay here. I might read a bit, or weed that neglected perennial garden on the side of the house."

"I'm sure the plants would thank you. Since I'm new at this yard thing, I have difficulty distinguishing between weeds and flowers. I'd do more harm than good trying to make it look presentable." Pushing away from the counter, Sam drained his mug, rinsed it and placed it in the dishwasher. "I'm going to shower, then I'll head out."

Three minutes after he disappeared down the hall, Cara heard the shower being turned on, followed by the sound of splashing water. The noise spoke of familiarity, of lives shared, reminding her of moments when she'd risen on tiptoe to steal a kiss as Sam emerged from the steamy bathroom, his hair damp, his eyelashes spiky with moisture.

Abruptly, she stood and switched on the radio, cranking up the volume. But even when she'd turned it as high as she dared, she couldn't quite eliminate the sound of running water—or the unexpected yearning it evoked.

Eight hours later, when Sam pulled into his driveway after a trip to Rolla and an unexpectedly busy day at the clinic, he noted that Cara had followed through on her plans to weed the side garden, unearthing a startling display of color in the process. Yellow day lilies turned sunny faces to the sky, bright pink peonies waved a greeting in the gentle breeze and purple flowers he couldn't identify peeked through heart-shaped foliage.

As he studied her handiwork, Sam recalled a discussion early in their marriage, when they were deciding where to live. Cara had preferred a house in the suburbs, with trees and gardens and a porch swing. Turned off by the prospect of annoying maintenance problems and an inconvenient commute, he'd quashed the idea. She hadn't pushed, and he'd all but forgotten about it.

Now, as he stared at the lovingly tended garden, he was faced with yet another example of his selfishness. So often in their marriage Cara had bowed to his wishes when he'd brushed hers aside. Not out of weakness, but love.

He couldn't remember one occasion when he'd done the same for her.

Gripping the wheel, Sam bowed his head, resting his forehead on his hands. And found himself turning in desperation once again to the God he'd also brushed aside.

Lord, I used to think I could handle things on my own. That I was invincible. I don't anymore. The past couple of years have been a wake-up call. I know I don't have the right to ask for Your help after being a stranger for such a long time, but I have a feeling that You sent Cara back into my life to give me one last chance to mend our marriage. If that's true, please…please help me undo the damage I've caused.

Easing his foot off the brake, Sam continued toward the detached garage. As he approached the house after retrieving his mail, he took care to alert Cara of his arrival by being noisier that necessary. He also called out to her from the living room.

When there was no response, he headed for the kitchen, which was once again filled with savory aromas. Cara wasn't there but he did notice something important.

There were two places set at the table.

Before he had a chance to process the significance of that she stepped into the hall from her bedroom.

"I thought I heard you come in." Her color was higher than usual, and she hesitated at the end of the corridor.

"The house smells good." He nodded toward the table from the kitchen doorway. "Expecting company?" There was no sense pretending he hadn't seen the two place settings.

Crossing her arms over her chest, she shifted her weight. "I've been thinking about it, and I...I cook anyway. It doesn't make sense not to prepare enough for two. Taking care of our own meals sounded okay in theory, but it seems kind of silly in practice. Unless you'd rather leave things as they are."

"No." His response was so quick that she gave him a startled look. Struggling to contain his delight, he modulated his voice. "You're right. This is more logical. And I won't lie. Giving up Gus's is no great sacrifice."

A smile whispered at her lips. "Then dinner's ready whenever you are."

"Give me five minutes."

She waited at the end of the hall until he entered his bedroom, moving only after he stepped inside. It was clear that she wanted to keep her distance. In a physical sense, at least. But the door had just been cracked at another level, moving him closer to his goal.

And even if it was a tiny step, at least it was in the right direction.

Chapter Six

By Sunday, Cara was starting to go stir-crazy. Sam's house was a fine refuge, but in the past few days she'd read three books and cooked enough food to feed them both for the next week. Recalling Marge's invitation to attend church services, Cara was suddenly tempted to accept. Though she read her Bible every day, she missed worshipping with a faith community each week. There was something uplifting and energizing about joining with other believers in prayer and song.

The church Marge had mentioned was only a short distance away. A much shorter trip than her foray to Rolla for cooking supplies. Then again, that had been an emergency run, as far as Cara was concerned. She hadn't been tempted to do any further exploring. Until today.

As if to beckon her, a bell began to toll for the ten o'clock service. Why not give it a try? She could slip in the back, then slip out again if she became uncomfortable. What did she have to lose?

The decision made, Cara cleared her breakfast dishes

off the table and headed for her room to change into clothing more appropriate for Sunday services than shorts and a T-shirt. Sam had gone to visit a hospitalized patient in Rolla, and chances were she'd be back before he was. But she'd leave a note in case he returned first.

A nervous flutter in her stomach as she pulled on a pair of black slacks reminded Cara that her plan was risky. The few times she'd ventured out in Philadelphia she'd had to battle panic attacks whenever anyone got too close. She'd battled them in the airport en route to Oak Hill, too, as the crowd pressed in on her from all sides. And people would be close in church, as well. Shoulder to shoulder in the pews. But she had to venture out alone sooner or later, and what could be safer than the house of God?

Fifteen minutes later, however, Cara's confidence wavered as she pulled into the parking lot beside the small white church, staring through the windshield at the tall steeple that soared toward the cloudless blue sky. Already her heart was beginning to pound, and a tremor shook her hands as a wave of fear swept over her. This was a mistake. She needed to get back to Sam's house, where she felt safe.

As she fumbled to put the car into Reverse, a sudden tap on her window startled her, and she jerked her head that direction. A smiling Marge stood on the other side, dressed in white slacks topped by a tie-dyed top that looked like a throwback to the 1970s.

Fighting to control her panic, Cara considered her options. If she ignored the innkeeper and left, tales of such odd—and rude—behavior would spread around town, raising questions and speculations that could put Sam in an awkward position. Not a good choice. Better to explain to Marge that she wasn't feeling well, and imply that she might see her next Sunday. That should work.

Lowering her window, Cara opened her mouth to speak. But Marge beat her to it.

"I'm so glad you came today, Cara. I've been wondering how you've been doing. Now that you're settled in, I hope we'll see more of you around town. And this is a good place to start. I know everyone in the congregation and I can introduce you at the coffee hour after services. We'll sit together, since you're by yourself. Too bad you couldn't get Dr. Martin to come with you. I've been working on him, but he's a stubborn man. Maybe if we team up we'll have better luck. Come along, now. We don't want to be late. The first hymn is always real rousing. Gets things off to a great start."

Before Cara could protest, Marge pulled open the car door and waited with an expectant expression.

She could still make an excuse and leave, Cara assured herself. No one could force her to attend services. But as the first chords of the organ echoed in the quiet air, her resolve wavered. She wanted to go back to church. She'd missed it with an intensity that had surprised her. And who better to clear the way than the dynamo beside her? She had a feeling Marge would stick to her like glue, smoothing out any rough spots.

Giving up the fight, Cara stepped out of the car and locked it.

"Now, that's something you don't have to worry about here." Marge chuckled as she linked her arm with Cara's. "There's no lawbreaking to speak of in Oak Hill. Dale Lewis, our sheriff, sees to that. And Abby

Warner, the editor of the *Gazette*, is a real crusader against crime and injustice. Between the two of them, we're in good hands."

By the time Marge finished speaking, she and Cara were halfway down the center aisle of the church, the older woman's arm still linked with hers. Alone, Cara would have been uncomfortable with the curious glances aimed her way. But Marge's presence served as a balm to her nerves. And after they slipped into a pew and the service began, Cara's tension eased. There was an almost tangible spirit in the congregation that she found comforting, and the words of Scripture proclaimed from the pulpit stirred her soul, as they always did. Marge's assessment of Reverend Andrews was also accurate. He seemed like a nice man, and Cara found his quiet, unassuming preaching style appealing.

When Marge once more commandeered her arm after the last hymn had been sung, Cara didn't panic. She was relaxed and more than willing to join the older woman for the coffee hour.

The spacious hall downstairs was already filled with chatter and laughter when they stepped inside. Marge worked the room with the polish of a politician, leading Cara from group to group, lingering long enough to exchange a few pleasantries before disengaging to head for the next cluster of people. Cara allowed herself to be guided around the hall, admiring Marge's consummate skill.

Cara met the famous Gus, a bald, rotund gent who looked as if he'd eaten a few too many of his own fried specials. Sheriff Dale Lewis, with his charming blond-haired daughter, Jenna, in tow, took her hand in a firm grip, his steel-blue eyes softening in welcome. Abby Warner seemed too young to be the crusading journalist Marge had described, but her smile was warm and welcoming. Reverend Andrews, with his open, pleasant face, invited her back for future services.

It wasn't difficult to deflect the discreet questions that were directed her way, and Cara felt as if she learned far more than she revealed. Including quite a bit about the townsfolk's perception of Sam. While he was liked and respected, it was clear from various comments that he kept to himself.

"Such a nice man. A bit of a loner, but a great doctor," one older man told her.

"We were happy to get him. Excellent credentials. Too bad he keeps to himself. Must be a lonely life." This from a young woman with a toddler clinging to her leg.

"I was so surprised when I heard you were coming," another woman remarked. "Dr. Martin never talks about his past. We saw his wedding ring, of course, but we thought he might be a widower."

While Cara was grateful that Marge kept them on the move, eliminating the possibility of any in-depth discussions, she wouldn't have minded following up on some of those remarks with a few questions of her own. But Marge had other plans. She seemed determined to introduce Cara to every single person in the church hall.

When they'd completed their circuit, ending up back by the door, Cara took a deep breath and smiled at the older woman. "Wow. That was amazing. Have you ever considered running for mayor?"

The suggestion seemed to appall Marge. "I don't want any part of politics. It's a messy business. Besides, the inn and my chamber of commerce work keep me plenty busy. I already get up with the chickens to cook breakfast for my guests. I sure don't want to be gadding about at night from one civic meeting to another, pushing an agenda and glad-handing. It's early to bed for me."

"So the inn doesn't serve dinner?"

Her comment had been nothing more than small talk, but a caution flag sprang up in Cara's mind when a sudden, speculative expression narrowed Marge's eyes.

"Goodness, no. I'm not a chef. Breakfast taxes my skills to the limit. But if I could find someone who was interested in taking that on, dinner might not be a bad idea. Oak Hill could benefit from a classy restaurant. The inn, too. It would draw people from miles around." Marge tilted her head and regarded Cara. "You aren't by any chance between jobs, are you?"

"No. I'm on temporary leave." Cara emphasized the word *temporary*. Feeling as if she'd opened a can of worms, and deciding that a fast exit was in order, she checked her watch. "I ought to get home. I expect Sam will be back soon." Not that it mattered. They had no plans to do anything together. But Marge didn't need to know that.

"Of course." She patted Cara's arm. "I think having you around will be good for Dr. Martin. He could use a little lightening up. I know big-city doctors move people in and out fast, but folks here expect to chat a little, like they did with old Doc Adams. He always took the time to talk, to let people know he cared, and everybody loved him for it. You might want to pass that on to Dr. Martin while you're here, you two still being friendly and all."

As Sam had told Cara the first night, describing their relationship as friendly stretched the truth. But again, Marge didn't need to know that. "I don't have a whole lot of influence," she demurred.

"Oh, I don't know. Maybe more than you think. If Dr. Martin didn't care what you thought, I doubt he would have spent hours painting that room or scouring the countryside for the perfect antique dresser."

"He painted the room himself?" Cara stared at Marge.

"Yes. I have it on good authority from Fred at the hardware store, where Dr. Martin bought the supplies. And Lacey Johnson at the antique store in Hanson's Grove told me that Sam stopped in to look at dressers. Spent two hours inspecting the merchandise before he settled on one."

Too surprised to respond, Cara continued to gape at Marge.

"Still waters run deep, you know. The trick is finding a way to tap into them." Marge chuckled and patted her arm. "You take care now, Cara. And I'll be in touch. I want to think about that restaurant idea."

As Cara exited the church hall and wandered back to her car, she realized that not once in the past two hours had she experienced even the hint of a panic attack. Thanks to Marge, who'd stuck close…and given her plenty to think about. Plus, she felt better than she had in weeks. Her self-imposed isolation in Philadelphia had helped her cope with the trauma of the shooting, but she wasn't by nature a solitary person. She liked people, was energized by new places and experiences. And today she'd taken a first step back into the world.

She'd also learned a few things about Sam. It didn't surprise her that he was having a problem adjusting to small-town family practice, given his poor communication skills. Once, in the early days of their relationship, Cara had thought he was learning to come out of his shell, to open up. She couldn't have married him if he hadn't. Though there had been a spark between them from their first meeting, she'd known that chemistry alone wouldn't be enough to sustain a relationship over the long term. There had to be a connection at other levels as well—spiritual, emotional and intellectual.

And there had been, in the beginning. Difficult as it had been for him, Sam had found the courage to open his heart and trust her. To share his dreams, his hopes, his successes—as well as his disappointments and failures. That was when she'd fallen in love with him, when attraction had blossomed into something far deeper and more lasting.

But as their careers had taken off and ambition mushroomed, the closeness they'd developed ebbed away. And their rift had been compounded by Sam's anger and bitterness after the attack. Cara had withdrawn, and Sam had…

No. She wasn't going to go there, Cara admonished herself as she climbed into her car and headed back toward the house. It was ancient history. The past couldn't be changed.

Yet people could, she acknowledged, considering the apparent changes in Sam—the very changes she'd once hoped time and reflection would trigger. Gone was the hard edge of arrogance, along with his cynicism and bitterness. He seemed to have at last accepted the hand he'd been dealt and was doing his best to make the transition from surgeon to family practitioner. No matter her personal feelings toward him, she respected him for trying.

Had she met Sam now, Cara mused, she might once again be drawn to him. He'd shown her nothing but kindness and consideration since her arrival, offering her an appealing glimpse of the man he'd once been, back in the days when their love was new and filled with promise. When she'd believed that her devotion would draw out the very best in the man to whom she'd entrusted her heart.

She'd been wrong about that.

Ironically, however, it seemed adversity had succeeded where she had failed.

As Cara parked beside the garage and walked toward the back porch, that conclusion was reinforced. Sam stood by the railing, a screwdriver in his hand, an uncertain smile hovering around his lips.

"My porch needed some furnishing, and I remembered that you once told me a house wasn't complete without a porch swing. I figured this might be a good addition."

Cara had no trouble recalling that conversation. But the fact that Sam remembered it astounded her. Speechless, she peeked around him to the swing he'd hung.

"Why don't you take the inaugural ride?"

Forcing her legs to carry her forward, she covered the distance between them. As she scooted onto the wooden slats that formed the seat, Sam moved behind her and gave a gentle push.

The steady, smooth rhythm was a balm for her unsettled nerves. Clutching her Bible in her lap, she closed her eyes, letting the warm morning breeze caress her face.

"Looks like it gets the stamp of approval."

Her eyelids flickered open. Sam had moved to the porch railing and was leaning against one of the support beams. The tender look in his eyes stole the breath from Cara's lungs. "It's perfect. Just like the one I had when I was growing up."

"I'm glad you like it." He stuck the screwdriver in his pocket and gestured toward her Bible. "I didn't expect you to venture out to church already."

She ran a finger over the worn cover. "I almost didn't make it. I got as far as the parking lot and decided to come back."

"Why didn't you?"

"Marge appeared at my window. The next thing I knew, she had me by the arm and we were walking down the aisle."

"That sounds like Marge." A chuckle rumbled deep in Sam's chest. "I hope I have half her energy when I'm her age. How was the service?"

"Good. I felt much more peaceful afterward. You ought to try it sometime."

"I just might do that."

His response surprised her, but he pushed away from the wooden column and turned toward the house before she could speak. "Enjoy the rest of the day while you can. We're supposed to get a storm later."

Watching the door shut behind him, Cara recalled a

comment Marge had made at church. Still waters run deep. That phrase had always applied to her husband, Cara acknowledged. His actions since her arrival in Oak Hill demonstrated that, suggesting that he still cared. That he wanted to make amends. That he regretted what he'd done to destroy their marriage.

Yet he hadn't spoken the words. And true communication involved both words and deeds. Whether he could overcome that problem remained to be seen.

But what if he did? What if he told her he was sorry? Asked her for another chance to prove his love? Promised to make things right? What then?

The answers to those questions eluded Cara. Besides, even if that scenario came true, there were formidable obstacles to a reunion. And the biggest one, she knew, lay in her.

.How did one forgive betrayal?

The weight of the Bible in her hands reminded her that she had to look no further than Jesus for an answer to *that* question. As He'd hung on the cross, an innocent man unjustly accused, he'd forgiven His unrepentant killers and asked His Father to do the same. Shouldn't it be far easier to forgive a husband who expressed remorse and was eager to mend the rift? Yet it wasn't.

So much for being a good Christian, Cara conceded.

Running her fingers over the smooth oak boards of the swing as she moved back and forth, Cara wondered if she was reading too much into Sam's kindness. Maybe he was motivated by guilt over the pain he'd caused her. Maybe he considered her interlude at his house his penance, and he had no interest in getting back together on a permanent basis. For all she knew, he was dating again.

Yet, in her heart, Cara didn't think so. Sam had never been a womanizer. Once they'd become serious, he'd admitted to her that until she'd come along, he'd had to rely on well-meaning acquaintances to arrange dates. And she doubted that had changed. In a town the size of Oak Hill, most people would know if he was seeing someone. And she'd have heard about it today. Instead, people thought of Sam as a loner—and lonely.

Cara knew all about being lonely. And she also knew that loneliness wasn't reason enough to consider reconnecting with someone who had caused her heartache—even if the man was interested. And repentant.

No, a reconciliation would have to be motivated by a lot more than that.

But even if it was, a reunion would still be far too risky.

Chapter Seven

For the first time since her arrival in Oak Hill, Cara had trouble sleeping. Sam's earlier prediction that bad weather was on the way turned out to be accurate, and flashes of lightning followed by house-shaking booms of thunder had been disrupting her sleep for almost an hour. Bleary-eyed, she squinted at the digital display on the clock radio on her nightstand. Two in the morning.

Resigned to wakefulness, at least until the storm abated, Cara replayed the events of the day in her mind. Following their short exchange on the porch, Cara hadn't seen much of Sam. She had no idea what his usual Sunday routine consisted of, but today he'd stayed sequestered in his office while she'd put the porch swing to good use, enjoying a gripping suspense novel.

Dinner had been his incentive to emerge and, during the meal, he'd attempted to engage her in conversation, keeping things light as he did every night. The awkwardness of the situation was difficult to overcome, but she admired him for trying. And as he'd done each evening they'd dined together, he'd insisted on cleaning up. Another first in their relationship.

The changes in Sam continued to impress Cara. While the low point in their marriage—that fateful night in the movie theater parking lot—had destroyed Cara's trust and hopes of salvaging their relationship, it seemed to have been a turning point for him.

She'd only been in Oak Hill a week, however, and their contact had been limited. Anyone could be nice for a few days. Sustaining that kindness and consideration week after week, month after month, year after year, was the true test of love. One they'd failed in the past.

And Cara had no confidence they'd pass if given a second chance.

The faint ringing of a phone nudged Cara awake. When the storm had at last subsided a little before three, she'd drifted back to sleep. But deep slumber had eluded her, leaving her attuned to the slightest of noises. A ringing phone, however muffled, brought her awake at once.

Halfway into the second ring, the phone went silent, as if it had been snatched from its cradle. Cara listened, alert, as she checked the clock in the darkness. Four-thirty. When she heard nothing more, her eyelids grew heavy. But the sound of a door being softly closed a few minutes later brought her awake again.

Panic gripped her, and Cara scrambled out of bed. Padding over to her door, she eased it open and peered down the hall to find Sam heading for the kitchen. He wore black slacks and a white oxford shirt, and he carried a black bag.

"Sam?"

Her tentative question halted him mid-stride, and he turned. "Sorry to wake you, Cara. I grabbed the phone as fast as I could."

"Is something wrong?"

"One of my patients has pneumonia, and he won't let me put him in the hospital. His wife just called to tell me that he's having difficulty breathing, but he doesn't want her to call an ambulance. I need to go out there."

"You make house calls?" Cara stared at him. Doctors didn't do that anymore, did they?

"Only in emergencies. It doesn't happen very often."

"H-how long will you be gone?"

The tremor in Cara's voice reminded Sam of her fear of being alone in the dark. He couldn't see her face in the shadows, but her rigid body posture, and her grip on the door, suggested that his departure had stoked those fears.

"It's about a twenty-five-minute drive each way. I'm not sure how long I'll be there. Would you like to ride along, since you're awake anyway?" Sam expected Cara to turn him down at once. But to his surprise, she hesitated.

"Wouldn't your patient think that was pretty odd?"

"You could wait in the car when we get there. It's warm enough, and the Johnsons live on a farm so there's nobody around for miles. They don't need to know you came along."

Torn, Cara debated. She was safe in Sam's house. And in less than an hour, it would be light. Yet she couldn't stem the panic that clutched at her lungs, squeezing the air out of them. The fear was irrational, she knew that. But she also knew that she couldn't control it. If she stayed home alone, the panic attack could escalate, as had often happened in the past few weeks. Already tired from her restless night, she wasn't up to dealing with the havoc that it would wreak on her.

"If you're sure it would be okay, I can be ready in five minutes."

"I'll wait for you in the kitchen."

Four and a half minutes later, Cara found him by the back door. She'd thrown on a pair of jeans and a T-shirt, and run a brush through her hair. Already she was feeling foolish about her cowardice, yet the notion of staying alone in the dark house freaked her out.

If Sam thought her behavior irrational, however, he was kind enough to keep his opinion to himself. In silence she preceded him out the door, hovered close while he locked it, and was grateful when he placed a protective hand in the small of her back as they walked through the still, early-morning darkness toward the garage.

Depositing his case in the backseat of the car, he opened her door, then took his place behind the wheel. Neither spoke until he backed out and headed away from town on a small country road. At that point, feeling more foolish by the minute, Cara felt compelled to say something. The inky darkness around them hid their expressions, making it easier to share confidences.

"Ever since the shooting, I've…had difficulty dealing with darkness." Her voice was soft in the quiet car, not much louder than the background hum of the engine. "I know it's silly, but I can't seem to help it. I hope it isn't too awkward for you that I came along."

Awkward didn't come close to describing how Sam viewed this outing. *Providential* would be a better word. Since Cara had arrived a week ago, he'd been desperately trying to think of ways to increase their time together without infringing on the turf she'd delineated. That she'd suggested sharing dinner had been an unexpected—and most welcome—gift. One that had boosted his feeble hopes and given him the courage to invite her to drive to Rolla with him. But her refusal of that invitation had dimmed those hopes. Since then, he'd come up with no other plan to convince her to spend more time with him. Yet once again, an opportunity had been dropped in his lap.

The silence had lengthened, and Sam realized he owed her a response. Or better yet, a reassurance. "It's not awkward at all. In fact, I appreciate the company. It's a long drive in the dark alone."

Quiet descended on the car again as Sam tried to think of some way to extend the conversation. But for once, Cara took the lead.

"I didn't think doctors made house calls anymore."

"It seems country doctors do. At least Doc Adams did, as I've been told by countless patients. I figured he'd be a hard act to follow when I took over his practice, and I was right."

"Marge said he was well liked."

"Yeah. He was a good man."

"How did you two connect?"

"He and Dad went to medical school together, and they never lost touch. I'd met him on a few occasions through the years. Somehow he heard about my...about what happened…and he got in touch. We talked several times, and he ended up offering to sell me his family practice. He was getting ready to retire and wanted to bring in someone he trusted, who could build on the tradition of compassionate care he'd created."

Sam hesitated for a few moments, and when he continued his discouraged tone tugged at her heart. "To be honest, I often think he could have done better. If he hadn't died a month after he retired, I might have suggested he find a better candidate to carry on his legacy."

The cover of darkness seemed to have given Sam the courage to open up a bit, too, Cara noted. "I have a feeling you're being too hard on yourself. If you didn't care, you wouldn't be making a house call miles away in the wee hours of the morning."

"This trip is a reflection of my failure, not my benevolence, Cara. I tried to convince Marv Jackson to let me admit him to the hospital when he came into my office two days ago. I failed. Doc Adams would have succeeded."

Hearing his frustration, Cara recalled Marge's comment about Sam needing a little lightening up. And the remarks from congregants about him being a loner, and keeping to himself. Knowing Sam, Cara assumed that he'd used a very logical, clinical approach with Marv Jackson. That had always been his style as a surgeon, where patient/doctor relationships were short-term and straightforward and the focus was on a very specific job that needed to be done.

In family practice, however, doctors had to treat the whole patient, over the long term. To do that well they needed to develop a caring relationship based on trust and understanding. The kind Doc Adams had created, which made the patient receptive to a doctor's recommendation, however distasteful it might be.

Unable to dispute Sam's response, Cara fell silent. She couldn't ignore the evidence that suggested he had a problem relating to patients. Nor was she surprised by his dilemma, knowing him as well as she did. Yet it was clear he wanted to succeed. But she wasn't sure he would, not without guidance. As to who could provide that…she wasn't going to go there.

They completed the ride in silence. Not until Sam pulled into the long, gravel lane leading to a frame, two-story farmhouse did he speak. "I'll park on the side. That way no one will know you're here. I'll lock the doors, but lean on the horn if anything spooks you. To be honest, though, about the only thing likely to bother you out here is a cow or a goat."

At his teasing tone, Cara's lips twitched in response. For some reason, she wasn't all that worried about waiting in the dark car. The locks and the horn helped, as did the rural setting. Besides, there was already a subtle glow on the eastern horizon. All symptoms of her earlier, impending panic attack had vanished.

"I'll be fine. Don't worry about me."

With a nod, Sam got out of the car, opened the back door and reached for his bag. "I'll be back as soon as I can."

"Sam."

His name came out before she could stop it, and her neck grew warm as he leaned down again, a question in his eyes. She hadn't intended to offer any advice; yet she'd been touched by his admission that he'd failed to convince the ill man in this house to get the necessary medical care. And an idea had occurred to her. Taking a deep breath, she plunged in.

"I was just thinking about that time you twisted your ankle and refused to get it looked at. You thought it was a sprain. But it turned out to be a fracture, and because you didn't get it treated right away, there were complications. Maybe if you tell that story to Marv Jackson, it might help convince him that things could get worse if he doesn't go to the hospital. Sometimes sharing a personal experience makes people more receptive."

The dim overhead light in the car did little to illuminate Sam's face. But Cara was sure she saw a flicker of some indefinable emotion, some subtle shift in his features. "I'll keep that in mind. Thank you."

And then he was gone.

Forty-five minutes later, as the sun crested the horizon and cast a golden glow over the green fields, the flash of another light caught Cara's attention. An ambulance had turned into the gravel driveway.

It seemed Sam had won his case.

From her position at the side of the house, Cara watched as the EMTs exited the vehicle. A few minutes later they came back and removed the gurney. Ten minutes after that, they were securing it on board, the older man lying on top already hooked to an IV. The ambulance departed, followed by a car. Sam joined her a short while later, stowing his case in the back and slipping into his seat.

In daylight, Cara could see the lines of fatigue at the corners of his eyes. But his lips were smiling. "It worked." He turned the key in the ignition and eased the car down the long driveway.

"You told him about your ankle?"

"Yes. In all the gory details. Including how stubborn I was, and how I ignored my wife's advice—and the price I paid. For some reason, knowing that I'd been stupid seemed to compel him not to want to make the same mistake. He even shook my hand. I've never had a patient in Oak Hill do that."

"I'm glad things worked out."

"Thanks to you." He risked a quick look at her, then focused again on the road. "I think this calls for a celebration. And I have the perfect thing in mind."

Curious, she examined his profile, warmed by the morning light. "What?"

"It's a surprise. If you're game."

"Sure." She had no plans for the day, other than a nap later to compensate for her disrupted sleep. Rolling down her window a few inches, she leaned back in her seat, enjoying the fresh scent of a country morning and the song of the birds as they trilled in the quiet air. Sam, too, seemed content to drive in silence.

Fifteen minutes later they entered a tiny town, and Sam pulled to a stop in front of a storefront with a sign marked Sweet Stuff.

"The best bakery for miles around." Sam opened his door. "I discovered it a few months ago after another early-morning call in this area, and I try to get back every few weeks. The owners are from

Denmark, and their Danish pastry is the best this side of the Atlantic."

A few minutes later he was back, toting a white paper sack and a cardboard tray containing two cups of coffee. He reached in and handed the goodies over to Cara before sliding back in. "If you can resist the aroma for a few minutes, I know the perfect place to enjoy this."

"I'm not sure I can hold off." As Cara inhaled, the scent of fresh-baked pastry set off a rumble in her stomach.

"You always did have a sweet tooth." He shot her a grin. "I never could figure out how you stayed so slender."

"Working in a kitchen burns up a lot of calories."

The skeptical look he gave her was one thing that hadn't changed about him, she realized. Sam never had understood that the grueling pace of a commercial kitchen was as physically taxing as surgery. She'd given up trying to convince him of that long ago. And now wasn't the time to reopen that sore subject. Ignoring his look, she lifted the flap on the bag and peeked in. The pastries did look authentic. Her mouth began to water. "How much farther?"

"About half a mile."

As Sam rounded a curve in the road a minute later, he eased onto a small gravel pull-off at the top of a hill. Framed by large oak trees, it offered a panoramic view. As the rising sun played hide-and-seek with the fluffy white clouds strewn about the blue sky, mischievous rays darted toward the ground, turning a meandering stream into a silver ribbon. When Sam shut off the engine and lowered his window, the peace was absolute except for the morning song of the birds.

"Wow." Cara breathed, rather than spoke the word, enchanted by the scene in front of her.

While she drank in the landscape, Sam traced her profile with a loving gaze. Despite her lack of makeup and hastily brushed hair, she was still the most beautiful woman he'd ever met. But her beauty wasn't just physical. From the beginning, he'd recognized her loveliness of spirit and kindness of heart, realized that there was depth and purpose and character to Cara.

Yet somewhere along the way, in the frenzy of success and professional adulation, he'd ceased to appreciate the qualities that made her such a special woman. All that had mattered was his career.

Despite his neglect, however, she'd stuck with him. Even when he'd given her nothing but abuse, she'd tried to be there for him. Far longer than he'd had a right to expect. Only his final indiscretion had driven her away.

Smiling, Cara opened the sack and turned to Sam. "I can't wait any…"

The words died in her throat and, with a sinking feeling, Sam watched as wariness—and fear—wiped away her smile. Struggling to compose his features, he did his best to erase any visible trace of what was in his heart. He wanted Cara to know that he hoped for a reconciliation, but the time wasn't yet right for that revelation. Not when she was still dealing with her own trauma. And not until she had a chance to discover for herself that he'd changed.

"Are you going to share those?" He gestured toward the bag and tried for a teasing inflection.

"Sure." She dug into the sack and extracted some napkins and one of the flaky pastries.

He reached for it with both hands, and their fingers brushed. She snatched hers back.

"Your hand…seems better." She buried her face in the sack again as she selected a pastry for herself.

"Not better. But improved."

To Cara's surprise, there was no bitterness in his matter-of-fact tone, and she sent him a curious look. His placid, relaxed expression bore no trace of the intimate warmth and caring she'd glimpsed moments ago, when for a brief instant tenderness had softened his features and the yearning in his eyes had stolen the breath from her lungs. Now she wondered if she'd imagined it. "You sound okay with that."

"Resigned, anyway." He took a bite of the pastry, and she watched as pieces of the outer layer of dough flaked off and drifted to the napkin he'd spread on his lap. They reminded her of autumn leaves, falling one by one, leaving the trees bare and exposed. "At least I regained enough use to stay in medicine. Although I often wonder if that was a good thing. I was a far better surgeon than family practitioner. Surgery requires coordination and dexterity. Family practice requires communication and discernment. Those have never been my strong points."

He started to take another bite of his pastry, then changed his mind. Setting it on his lap, he turned to her, his eyes bleak. "I guess our marriage proves that."

The raw anguish on his face tightened Cara's throat. "There was fault on both sides, Sam."

"That's not true." He tightened his grip on the cup and drew a harsh breath. "I take full responsibility for what happened between us."

"I was just as wrapped up in my job as you were in yours." Looking down, Cara traced the rim of her cup with one finger. "Relationships can't survive without nurturing, and neither of us devoted enough attention to that after our careers took off."

"But you recognized it, and were willing to try and fix it. I wasn't."

She couldn't argue with that.

"Besides, I'm not sure that alone would have driven us apart. It's what I did after the attack that killed our marriage." He set his coffee back into the cup holder, and out of the corner of her eye Cara could see that his hands were trembling. "I want you to know how sorry I am for pushing you away. And I also want you to know that…" He stopped and cleared his throat, then laid his scarred fingers on the back of her hand, his touch gentle, tentative.

Startled, she stopped breathing. When she risked a peek at him, he caught—and held—her gaze.

"Despite what it looked like that night, Cara, nothing happened."

That night.

He didn't have to spell it out. The night she and Liz had run into Sam in a movie theater parking lot, a young blond clinging to his arm, was forever etched in her memory. It had been the most profound blow she'd ever sustained.

Yet even after being confronted with the evidence of his infidelity, Cara had found it hard to believe that Sam would betray her. She'd had absolute trust in him through all the years they'd lived together as man and wife, sure that despite their problems, he would honor their marriage vows. But that night had shattered her trust. And without trust, they had a marriage in name only. That was when she'd walked out.

Searching his eyes now, however, Cara could see nothing but sincerity in their depths. Could he be telling the truth? Had the night in the parking lot been an aberration? The result of one too many solitary evenings spent at the local bar as he struggled to cope with his chaotic life? An attempt to find the consolation she'd withdrawn? An indiscretion born of desperation rather than an actual act of infidelity?

But there was more. She could see that he wanted to continue, yet something was holding him back. Unsure whether she wanted to hear the rest of his confession, she remained silent. If he was seeking absolution, she didn't think she was up to the task.

Shame coursed through Sam as he studied Cara. It was too soon to ask for her forgiveness, but he needed to put his contrition on the table. And that meant he had to be honest about everything. If she ever gave her pardon, it had to be for the whole ball of wax. Because wrong intentions were as immoral as wrong actions. However hard they were to confess.

Forcing himself to look her in the eye, Sam spoke again, his voice not quite steady. "What I said before was the truth, Cara. I've always been faithful to you. That night was the first time I'd ever…seen a woman socially…since I met you. And there's been no one since. But I'm ashamed to admit that if we hadn't run into you and Liz, I…I'm not sure I could make that statement. And I'm as sorry about that as if something had actually happened."

He lifted a hand to massage the taut furrows in his forehead. "I know it's no excuse, and I don't expect you to fully understand the depths of my despair, but hopelessness and depression led me to that night. It wasn't because I stopped loving you."

Although she didn't move a muscle, Sam felt her withdraw as surely as if she'd jerked her hand back and turned away. It was what he'd expected, yet the effect was no less devastating.

The ache in his heart, the sense of loss that had been with him since the day she'd left him, intensified in the silence. Her hand lay cold and still beneath his, and at last Sam forced himself to break contact. He supposed he'd rushed this discussion. But when the opportunity had presented itself, he'd taken it. Now he was sorry. It had been too soon to bring up the past. She hadn't been ready to listen, let alone forgive.

Even worse, maybe she never would be.

Putting the car in gear, he backed away from the serenity and promise of the scene below them, where a new day was dawning.

Neither spoke a word on the way home. When he pulled into the driveway, Cara got out of the car almost before it came to a stop and disappeared into her room, leaving him alone in the kitchen, the bag of Danish in one hand and a cup of coffee in the other.

He took a sip, hoping to dispel the chill in his heart. But the dark brew offered no comfort, for it too had grown cold.

Chapter Eight

❧

Marge was right. You couldn't miss the Oak Hill Inn.

As Cara pulled to a stop in front of the gingerbread-bedecked Victorian house, painted pale pink with deep rose-colored trim, her lips curved into an appreciative smile. Marge might not find the ornate style appealing, but Cara thought the house was nostalgic and charming. And it was just what she needed to distract her from her conversation with Sam over Danish, which was still replaying in her mind two days after it occurred.

Climbing the steps to the wraparound porch, Cara admired the artful arrangement of white wicker furniture and the graceful ferns that trailed from hanging baskets under the eaves and overflowed from numerous plant stands set on the wooden floor.

"I see you found the pink elephant."

At the sound of Marge's voice, Cara transferred her attention to the front door. Attired in bright green slacks and a harvest-gold V-necked tunic top, the hem edged with beaded, iridescent fringe, the innkeeper pushed open the screen door and grinned. "Come on in."

If Cara thought the outside of the house had evoked the nineteenth century, she felt as if she'd entered a time warp when she stepped inside. From the authentic period furnishings to the dark wood to the bric-a-brac accents, the interior looked as if it had been transported intact from the 1880s to the twenty-first century.

"Wow! This is amazing." Cara turned around three-hundred-and-sixty degrees in the foyer, trying to take it all in.

"I can think of other ways to describe it. High-maintenance, for one."

At Marge's long-suffering tone, Cara looked at her. "I imagine the upkeep is pretty intimidating."

The innkeeper gave an unladylike snort. "That's putting it mildly."

"Did you ever think about selling it?"

"I used to, when I first got here. But the place is kind of growing on me. Not that it will ever be my style, you understand."

No, it wouldn't be, Cara agreed, casting another discreet glance over Marge's attire.

"It does have a certain appeal, however. And my guests seem to love it. I've had people come from as far away as Atlanta to see the place. It has quite a history. Would you like a quick tour before we get down to business?"

"I'd love one."

Marge hadn't been kidding when she said quick, Cara realized, as they headed up the grand staircase. The woman swept from room to room upstairs like a whirlwind. Cara was left with an impression of meticulous, charming decor in the eight guest bedrooms.

Once back on the first floor, Marge led the way to a large parlor, joined by sliding doors to a spacious dining room furnished with small individual tables. Both rooms boasted fireplaces with elaborate marble mantels.

"My aunt had a large cherrywood dining table in here when I inherited the place," Marge told Cara, gesturing toward the dining room. "It was more authentic, but I cater to couples looking for a romantic getaway, and they prefer having breakfast together."

"What's back there?" Cara pointed to another set of closed sliding doors at the far end of the room.

"The library." Marge crossed the polished walnut floor and parted the doors. "It's kind of an odd location. I don't need the space, so I use it for storage. It's an impressive room, though."

The original large dining table stood in the center, surrounded by odds and ends of furniture. The walls were lined with floor-to-ceiling bookshelves, all filled with antique volumes. A bit smaller than the dining room, the library had a cozy ambiance. And the deep windows, with cushioned window seats, looked like the perfect place to spend a rainy afternoon.

"Well, that's the ten-cent tour." Marge closed the doors again. "And now, to the heart of the house."

Leading the way through a butler's pantry, Marge pushed open the door to the kitchen. And once more, Cara was impressed.

No effort had been made in this room to preserve the Victorian character. Stainless-steel appliances and commercial-grade dishwashers and sinks lined the perimeter, and a large stainless-steel prep station formed an island in the center. Off to one side, a small walk-out bay window had been transformed into a cozy dining nook complete with an oak table and chairs. Woven place mats on the table and a colorful bouquet of flowers in a pottery vase invited closer inspection.

Cara gave the working part of the kitchen an appreciative survey as Marge led the way to the table. "This is fabulous."

"It is something, isn't it?" Marge reached for a carafe of coffee and filled two big mugs as they took their seats. "I can't imagine why my aunt went to this kind of expense when all she did was serve breakfast for sixteen people in the morning. Less than that when the inn wasn't full...which is usually the case, except on weekends."

"Maybe she had plans to do more."

"Could be. But her health started to decline, and by the end I think she was lucky to be able to manage breakfast." Marge pulled a tablet toward her and picked up a pencil. "Now, let's get down to business. Why I agreed to chair the church's food booth at the community Fourth of July festival is beyond me. I'm more into health food and vegetarian fare than fried chicken. But when I tried to nix the chicken, I was told that it's sacrosanct.

"However, I've got some leeway on the sides. That's where I thought you might be able to help. The standard menu has been coleslaw, potato salad and green beans with bacon bits. Trust me, I'm open to other suggestions. And I'm running out of time."

As they tossed ideas back and forth, Cara considered

that a few days ago, very little could have pried her away from the safety of Sam's house. But since their conversation Monday morning over Danish pastry, Cara had done her best to avoid him. Was it possible she'd misinterpreted the brief tender look on his face before he shuttered it? Perhaps it had been no more than a simple play of light.

Yet she'd been uncomfortable ever since. With that, as well as his expression of remorse, which seemed to call for a response she wasn't ready to give. While they'd continued to eat dinner together, she always retreated to her room or the porch swing afterward. She was only able to relax when he was gone during the day.

However, since today was his day off, he'd be home for at least a few hours. Marge's call earlier in the week, requesting her assistance with the church booth at the Fourth of July festival, had given her a good excuse to leave the house without making it obvious that she was trying to steer clear of him.

An hour later, after hashing over various options, she and Marge had decided to supplement the fried chicken with Greek pasta salad, Mexican corn bread, chilled marinated vegetables and spiced apples. Cara had also agreed to supervise the preparation of the dishes in the church kitchen during the two days preceding the event.

"We're going to knock their socks off." Marge examined the menu, chortling. "The Oak Hill Fourth of July festival has never seen a menu like this!"

"People might prefer what they're used to."

"True. But playing it safe is boring. Sometimes people need to take chances, try new things. Explore one of those side roads I mentioned when we met. Besides, now that you've agreed to oversee all the preparation, I have every confidence this will be a huge hit. I must confess, I did a little checking on the Internet after church Sunday. Dr. Martin told me you were a chef, but I had no idea you were so accomplished."

Warmth stole over Cara's cheeks. She knew there were a number of articles about her floating around in cyberspace, since she'd been featured in several local and regional publications in the past couple of years. But she was surprised anyone in Oak Hill had seen them.

"Don't believe everything you read in the newspaper," she demurred.

"I don't know. Our *Gazette* is always a stickler for accuracy. Abby makes sure of that. And I have a feeling the stories I found about you are true, too. Which brings me to another idea I wanted to discuss." Marge set aside her tablet and fixed a keen eye on Cara. "Remember our conversation on Sunday, about serving dinner at the inn?"

A caution flag went up in Cara's mind. The conversation Marge referred to had consisted of a couple of sentences, all triggered by an innocuous comment made by Cara. But if she hadn't liked the gleam in Marge's eyes on Sunday, she liked it even less now.

"I recall asking if you served dinner." She gave the woman a wary look.

"And I said it might not be a bad idea. Now that I've given it some more thought, I think it's a great idea. I figured I could open up the library, use the big table for small groups, add some smaller tables around the walls. I have room for more tables in the dining room, too. All told, I think I could seat about fifty. And the kitchen could certainly handle that. Since I don't use those rooms at night anyway, it would be a perfect arrangement."

She leaned forward, excitement sparking in her eyes. "My thought is to serve dinner three nights a week, say Thursday, Friday and Saturday. Have a set menu and a single seating, about seven. Gourmet fare, with a midwestern accent, featuring local products whenever possible. I'm sure a concept like this would go over like gangbusters. There's nothing like it for miles around. What do you think?"

A bit overwhelmed by Marge's plans, Cara took a few seconds to digest the information. The idea seemed sound, and it would be a good use of the dining room and library in the evenings. Cara could picture the rooms, bathed in candlelight, soft music playing in the background, the tables covered with crisp linen. It would be a superb setting for a romantic dinner or a special-occasion meal.

"It sounds like an idea with great potential, Marge. But I thought you said you weren't a chef?" Cara lifted her mug to her lips.

"I'm not. But *you* are."

Cara had been afraid that was where Marge was heading. "I don't live here. Like I told you Sunday, I have a good job waiting for me in Philly."

"I know. But I got the impression from Dr. Martin that you'd be here for a few weeks, and I figured you might be willing to help me get this up and running."

"What about after I leave?"

"I'll have to hire a permanent chef. But I'm confident

I can find someone, because I plan to make a very attractive offer. Since weekend dinners are likely to bring in business for the inn as well, I'd leave the operation of the restaurant—the ownership, in fact—in the hands of the chef. In exchange for the space and the use of the kitchen, I'd just want a small percentage of the income. Seems like a fair deal to me."

It was more than fair, Cara agreed. And it was an arrangement she'd grab in a heartbeat if she planned to stay in Oak Hill. All her life, she'd yearned to open her own restaurant. But the long hours and financial commitment of such a venture had been too overwhelming.

With the kind of deal Marge was proposing, however, she would inherit an existing space and have limited hours of operation. The restaurant would provide a nice income without dominating her life. And she could follow her culinary instincts, experiment with ingredients, create her own signature dishes. The prospect was very appealing.

And completely out of the question. She was a visitor in Oak Hill, nothing more. This wasn't for her. And she wouldn't be here long enough to give Marge a great deal of help, much as she'd like to assist the woman.

"Opening a restaurant takes time, Marge. I doubt we'd get very far in a handful of weeks."

"Why not? The space exists. All we'd have to do is add a few more tables. The way you came up with the menu for the church booth, I don't expect you'd have much of a problem putting together a set menu three nights a week. After that, it's a simple matter of ordering the food and spreading the word. Being president of the chamber of commerce has its advantages, you know. It would be a piece of cake."

It was hard not to get caught up in Marge's enthusiasm. Starting up—and running—a restaurant, brief though it might be, would be a great experience. And it wasn't as if she had anything else to do while she was here. Besides, she missed cooking. Not to mention the fact that a project like this would give her an excuse to spend quite a few hours away from Sam's house.

There was one problem, of course. If they managed to get the restaurant up and running before she left, she'd have to go home at night at the end of the evening. If dinner was at seven, as Marge had suggested, she'd be finished far earlier than in a typical restaurant job… but not before dark. And she was still having problems with that.

Yet the town seemed safe. She felt comfortable here. If she wanted to restore normalcy to her life, she had to start going out at night alone sooner or later. What better place to test the waters than Oak Hill? She shouldn't let irrational fears stop her from taking advantage of this opportunity.

The more she considered it, the more enamored she became with Marge's suggestion. But she needed to think this through. Perhaps talk it over with Liz, who always offered sound advice.

"Why don't you give it some thought, Cara?" Marge spoke as if she'd read her visitor's mind. "I know it's a lot to take on. And since you're here for such a short stay, it might not be worth your while. But it could be fun."

Fun wasn't a word Cara had used much lately. But

she'd like to restore it to her vocabulary. And this would help. Gathering up her purse, Cara slung it over her shoulder and stood. "I'll think about it, Marge."

"Good. That's a start." The woman rose and walked with her toward the front door. "Meanwhile, I'll get all these ingredients ordered for the Fourth of July and alert the ladies at the church that they'd better be prepared to roll up their sleeves and learn a few new tricks. This will be their first experience working under a chef."

"I hope they won't resent me for barging in on their turf."

"You aren't barging in. I invited you. And I expect they'll be excited about it, once I share a few of your credentials with them. A Paris Cordon Bleu chef, no less! Oak Hill has finally hit the big time!"

Smiling in response to Marge's enthusiasm, Cara exited the inn and headed for her car. Not until she slid into the driver's seat, put her key in the ignition and pointed the car toward Sam's house did she manage to catch her breath.

Marge was amazing, no question about it. Despite her eccentric attire and whirlwind nature, the owner of the "pink elephant" was anything but scattered. With consummate skill and singular focus, she'd maneuvered Cara right where she wanted her. Not only had Cara signed on to oversee the church food booth, she'd agreed to consider helping Marge open a restaurant at the inn.

All of which confirmed the assessment Cara had made on Sunday.

Marge should have been a politician.

* * *

Later in the afternoon, Cara peered at her flushed face in the bathroom mirror. Even a tepid shower hadn't managed to cool her down. Philly could get warm, but she'd never experienced anything like the humid heat of Missouri. After working in the garden all afternoon, she felt like one of the wilted impatiens she'd rescued from the weeds on the side of the house. At least she didn't have to turn on the oven, since Sam had insisted on picking up dinner when he finished his volunteer stint at the rural clinic.

When she stepped into her bedroom, her gaze fell on the notes she'd jotted down after her meeting with Marge that morning. Cara hadn't planned to stay in Oak Hill more than four or five weeks, and she'd been in town ten days already. She doubted they'd be able to open before she left. But at least she could help with the planning. And the innkeeper was right; it would be fun.

After pulling on shorts and a sleeveless cotton blouse, Cara tried to tame her hair as she blow-dried it. Always full of natural curl, it had gone crazy in the Missouri humidity. So much for sleek sophistication, she reflected. Giving up the fight, she did her best to secure the unruly locks at her nape with a large barrette, although a few obstinate tendrils eluded her and curled around her face.

Retrieving her latest novel from the nightstand, Cara left her room and headed toward the back porch. If she could manage to catch a breeze on the swing, she'd pass the time until dinner out there. If it was too hot, she'd…

All at once, the pungent odor of garlic assailed her

nostrils, and Cara's step faltered. In a flash, she was transported back to the dark parking lot with Tony. Felt again warm breath on her cheek…cold metal pressed to her temple…strong arms holding her in a vise. Once more she heard the sound of harsh breathing close to her ear. Tasted the sharp tang of fear. Saw the anger and defiance in Tony's eyes. And knew with terrible certainty that there was a very good chance she was going to die.

Dizziness caught her unaware, and Cara dropped her book as she groped for the nearest door frame, trying to steady herself as the floor shifted beneath her feet. Her heart began to hammer in her ears, and she couldn't draw any air into her lungs. As the hall faded in and out of darkness, a wave of terror crashed over her.

Cara had had plenty of panic attacks since the shooting, but none this severe. And as fear gripped her throat, further restricting her airway, she knew she was about to pass out.

A soft thump in the hallway caught Sam's attention as he arranged the warm garlic bread in a basket. Cara must be ready for dinner. The shower had been running when he'd returned twenty minutes ago, but it had gone off soon after. He'd been expecting her to emerge any minute.

After a few seconds, when there was no further sound or sign of her, a warning bell sounded in his mind. Setting the bread on the table, he headed for the hall.

The sight that met his eyes stopped him cold. Cara was clutching the door frame leading to the hall bath, bent slightly, gasping for breath, an open book at her feet.

His adrenaline surging, Sam closed the distance

between them in a few long strides. When he grasped her shoulders, the tremors that shook her body shocked him. Other than an obvious weight loss and her unwillingness to stay alone at night, Sam had seen little evidence of her trauma since she'd arrived. That had changed in a heartbeat. She was in the throes of a full-fledged panic attack.

"Cara, you need to lie down. Let me help you." Despite his best effort to keep his voice low and calm, a quiver ran through it. He put his arm around her shaking shoulders, but when he tried to urge her toward the bedroom her legs buckled. Reacting on instinct, Sam bent and slipped his arm under her knees, then swung her into his arms. She seemed oblivious to his presence, her eyes wide with fear as she fought for air, her hands clenching and unclenching in spasms.

After laying her gently on the bed, Sam left her only long enough to grab his bag from the office. When he returned, he kept one eye on her rigid, shuddering body while he searched through his case. Extracting a small tablet, he eased it between her lips.

"This will help, Cara. Let it dissolve in your mouth. I'm here, and you're going to be okay." He took her ice-cold hand in a warm, firm clasp and began to stroke it, murmuring encouragement in a soothing voice. Though he'd had nightmares after his ordeal, he'd been spared panic attacks. But he'd studied them, just in case, and he knew how unpredictable and frightening they could be, how they could be triggered by the slightest cause— or no cause at all.

Unfortunately, there was little he could do to ease

Cara's immediate distress. The Niravam he'd given her was the quickest short-term remedy. Time was the best long-term cure, especially when the attacks were the result of a specific incident. In the interim, patients needed lots of understanding and emotional support to get through the debilitating episodes. He was more than willing to provide that.

The minutes seemed as long as hours while Sam waited for the medication to take the edge off Cara's panic. All the while, he continued to stroke her hand, her forehead, comforting her as best he could.

When at last the tension in her muscles began to ease and her breathing grew less arduous, she focused on him. Distress etched her features.

"S-sorry about this." Her voice was shaky and weak.

He smoothed the hair back from her damp forehead. "There's nothing to be sorry about, Cara. Panic attacks can't be controlled."

"I thought I was doing better. But that was one of the w-worst I've had."

Frowning, he cocooned one of her hands between his, noting the tremors that still ran through it. More from reaction than panic at this point, he deduced. Odd that she'd have one of her worst attacks this long after the shooting. Unless it had been triggered by something not obvious to him. "Do you have any idea what caused it?"

"Yes. The smell of garlic. When the robber g-grabbed me, I could smell the garlic on his breath. I thought he was going to k-kill us both." A sob escaped from her throat, and she covered her mouth with the knuckles of her free hand. "I'm sorry. This wasn't p-part of our agreement, and—"

"Cara," he cut her off, his tone firm but gentle. "I want to help, if I can. You don't need to apologize. And I'm the one who's sorry. I wouldn't have brought Italian food home if I'd known about the garlic."

"I should have mentioned it, I guess. But I didn't know I was going to react like this. And now I've ruined your dinner."

Food was the last thing on his mind. "It's not important. Why don't you rest a while? We'll eat later." He stood and reached for an afghan at the bottom of the bed, pulling it over her.

"Are you…will you be here?"

The uncertain, little-girl voice coming from the woman he'd always thought of as strong and confident tugged at his heart. "I'm not going anywhere. Just call if you need me. I'll be nearby."

And as Sam half closed the door behind him, he was more determined than ever to make that reassurance true not only for today, but for always.

It smelled like Christmas.

Two hours later, after an exhaustion-induced slumber, Cara paused on the threshold of her bedroom and sniffed the air, puzzled. The house was permeated by the scent of spruce, with a hint of bayberry thrown in for good measure. Her curiosity rising, she padded down the hall in her bare feet, grateful that on this trip her legs were far steadier than on the last. The deep sleep had restored her, and the only lingering effect from the panic attack was a pleasant one—the memory of Sam's warm hand gripping hers, and the soothing sound of his voice as he talked her back from the terror.

When Cara reached the end of the hall, she found the source of the holiday smells: a dozen scented candles, arrayed around the living room. The warm glow they created was comforting, but best of all they'd banished the odor of garlic. And now that she was closer to the kitchen, she caught a whiff of another aroma. It was soy-based—and appealing.

More curious than ever, Cara approached the door to the kitchen, stopping in stunned disbelief to take in a scene she'd never before encountered.

Sam was cooking.

And judging by the disarray in the kitchen, he'd been at it a while. No one could create a mess of that magnitude in less than an hour.

As if sensing her presence, Sam turned from scrutinizing an open book on the counter. After a quick assessment, the tension in his face eased. "You look better."

"But the kitchen doesn't."

Caught off guard by her teasing tone, Sam smiled. "I'm breaking in a cookbook I bought a year ago. Are you casting aspersions on my inaugural culinary foray?" He continued the banter, keeping the mood lighthearted.

"Not at all." She strolled into the kitchen and surveyed the damage. "Although this could qualify as a national disaster area."

Once upon a time, they'd enjoyed repartee like this, he recalled. It felt good to experience it again. "Hey, this is going to be a meal you'll never forget." He gave the frying pan on the stove a shake.

"That's what I'm afraid of."

He laughed outright, and Cara did, too—until he turned to her and their gazes connected. All at once her laughter faded.

Uncomfortable with the sudden coziness of the scene, she shifted her attention to the table and moved away from him. "Can I do anything to help?"

"It's almost ready. You could fill the water glasses, if you like."

She went about the task in silence for a minute before she spoke again. "What happened to the Italian food?"

"It's gone."

"You didn't have to do that, Sam."

"You may be sorry I did when you try this." He set plates of chicken stir-fry over rice on the table.

"It looks good." She took her place, venturing a glance his direction. "I appreciate the candles, too. I'm surprised you had something like that in the house."

"I found them in a closet when I moved in. Good thing I didn't pitch them." He sat, waiting for her to say her usual silent words of thanks.

Tonight, however, she surprised him by giving voice to her prayer as she bowed her head. "Lord, we're grateful to You for this meal. Help us always to recognize—and appreciate—Your many blessings. Thank you for friends and family who support us. Give us the courage and strength to persevere, and the wisdom to hear Your voice. And thank You for the small kindnesses we receive each day that brighten our lives. Amen."

As she draped her napkin on her lap, Cara knew that Sam was watching her. She sensed that her spoken prayer had surprised him, and that he was wondering about its meaning.

If he was looking to her to provide an answer, however, he was out of luck. The prayer had surprised her, too. She hadn't planned to speak it aloud, nor thought about its content. The words had come out of their own accord. Words that asked for guidance and expressed gratitude. Words that Sam could interpret with hope.

And that wasn't good. From their first phone conversation, Cara had suspected that Sam might view her visit as an opportunity to reestablish their relationship. She'd done her best to discourage him, tried to communicate that she wasn't interested in reconciling.

Because a reunion wasn't in her plans.

But considering the spontaneous prayer that had surprised both of them, she began to wonder if perhaps it *was* in God's plan.

Chapter Nine

As the bell for the ten o'clock service tolled the following Sunday, Sam gave himself a critical scan in the mirror behind his door, trying to dispel his nervousness. Although he hadn't stepped inside a church in years, he figured his khaki slacks, open-necked white shirt and navy-blue blazer would qualify as suitable attire. He was more worried about Cara's reaction when he suggested they attend together.

He wouldn't have had the courage to propose it, except her attitude toward him had softened a bit since her panic attack on Wednesday night. Their conversations at dinner had been less stilted, and instead of disappearing outside to the porch swing every night with a book, she'd stayed in the air-conditioned living room…mere steps away from the kitchen table, where he often caught up on professional journals. Close enough for him to cast discreet looks at her throughout the evening.

It hadn't taken him long to conclude that he could get used to her sharing his evenings.

To confirm that he *wanted* to get used to her sharing his evenings.

That was one of the reasons he'd decided to go back to church. It was becoming clearer to him each day that convincing his wife to put down roots in Oak Hill would require more influence than he could wield. Perhaps, if he gave the Lord some attention, the favor would be returned. It wasn't the most noble reason to go to church, he acknowledged, but at least he was honest about it.

As he heard Cara's door open, he was reminded of a second less-than-noble reason to attend church. It would give him another couple of hours in his wife's company. Another couple of hours to demonstrate to her that he was a changed man. He hoped the Lord would forgive him for that ulterior motive, too.

Summoning up his courage, he opened his door and stepped into the hall, greeting Cara with a tentative smile. "I thought I might join you today, if you don't mind."

Taken aback by the suggestion, Cara stared at Sam. Churchgoing had never been high on her husband's priority list. Why did he want to go now? To please her—or the Lord? But maybe it didn't matter, she reflected. In the old days, he'd gone to church to please her, too. She'd never objected, always holding out the hope that at some point, he'd make the faith connection for himself.

That had never happened. But a lot of things had changed since then. Perhaps now he'd be more receptive to the Lord's voice. And if going to church together—for whatever reason—helped him find his way back to his faith, how could she object…even if it felt awkward?

"Of course."

His smile relaxed a bit. "We can take my car."

A few minutes later, as they parked in the church lot and approached the entrance, Cara saw Marge standing by the front door. The older woman waved, and a pleased smile lit her face as they drew close.

"Well, isn't this nice!" she declared. "I was waiting for you, Cara, so you wouldn't have to sit alone. I'm happy to see you took care of that problem yourself."

A flush warmed Cara's neck. "It was Sam's idea to come."

"Of course it was. Dr. Martin, good to see you." Marge extended her hand, and when he took it she gave a hearty shake. "We're happy to have you. I told Cara the other day that I've been trying to get you to join us ever since you arrived. I'm glad to see that something—" her meaningful gaze flitted to Cara for a brief instant, "—convinced you to give us a try."

Before Sam could reply, Marge ushered them inside. "Take a seat anywhere. And I hope you'll stay for coffee afterward. I want to hear your latest thoughts on the restaurant idea, Cara. And the kitchen ladies have a couple of questions about the Fourth of July menu. I ordered the ingredients, and they're all set to start cooking on Tuesday."

Aware that Sam had cast a curious glance her way, Cara focused on pew selection. She hadn't mentioned either project to him, though she'd talked at length about them with Liz. Especially the restaurant idea. Her friend had urged her to get involved, backing up her reasoning with sound rationale—it would ease Cara back into the swing of working, take her mind off the trauma, get her creative juices flowing.

As always, the give and take with Liz had helped Cara clarify her thinking. And after additional reflection and prayer, she'd decided to assist the innkeeper. She'd planned to tell her today during the coffee hour, but she hadn't counted on Sam tagging along. Not that he'd stay for that, anyway. Social get-togethers weren't his thing.

Stopping at a pew about halfway down, Cara sent a questioning look toward Sam. When he nodded, she slipped inside.

Seated beside him in the quiet space, Cara once again admired the simple structure of the church, classic in design, with tall, clear windows that ran the length of each side. Electric brass candelabras hung over a center aisle that ended at the raised sanctuary, but their light was a mere flicker compared to the glorious morning sun streaming in the windows. The peaceful setting did much to restore Cara's calm, which had been shaken by Sam's unexpected company. She needed to focus on the service, she told herself. She was here to worship, not to think about the man beside her. Yet his presence a whisper away was hard to ignore.

Reverend Andrews's sermon helped, however. The man had an engaging style, conversational but compelling. Today, his theme was "Let not your hearts be troubled," and it was a message that resonated with Cara. In particular, the conclusion.

"Of all the gospel writers, John most emphasized love," the minister said. "And the placement of this reading is interesting—just preceding the Lord's passion and death…mere hours before He would part from those who had loved Him, and who had believed in Him enough to leave everything behind to follow Him. It is His final instruction to them, which emphasizes its importance. And the message is clear. 'Love one another as I have loved you. Put your trust in God, and in Me. Do not let your hearts be troubled, or be afraid.'

"In spite of the clarity of the Lord's message, His followers asked many questions that day. Until finally the Lord said, 'Have I been so long a time with you, and you have not known Me?' Imagine his frustration. He'd lived and worked with these people on a daily basis. Yet they still didn't understand who He was or what He was about. And when He died, they felt betrayed."

Reverend Andrews rested his hand on the Bible. "Of course, there is a happy ending to this story. The Lord's death wasn't the end, but the beginning. And in the weeks and months that followed, graced by the Holy Spirit, His disciples understood that and their faith was restored.

"But it isn't always that simple for us, is it? Yes, the Spirit is alive in our midst, but not in the dramatic way it was with the early disciples. And in a world rife with broken promises and betrayal, it can be very hard to follow His commandment to love one another as He loved us. In the face of hurt, our hearts often become troubled, and we're afraid."

The minister gazed out at the congregation, his expression kind. "John focused on love for a very good reason.

It's the basis of our faith. But love is an overused word in our society. Despite what the media might suggest, it's not contingent on appearance or power or prestige. Nor is it as shallow as the unsustainable excitement of new romance. True love is the day in, day out getting along. It's about sharing and sacrifice, about unselfishness and forgiveness. Not once, but over and over again."

Pausing, he rested his hands on the edges of the pulpit. "In our world today, we have no better example of this kind of love than a good marriage. But even in the best marriages, there are moments when husbands and wives can relate to the Lord's question to Philip, 'Have I been so long a time with you, and you have not known Me?' Yet somehow, they persevere. With trust, and with faith, and with hope. Just as the Lord instructed us to do with Him.

"Today, let us resolve to imitate that example and to live the instructions our Lord gave His followers the night before He died. Love one another, trust in God, and free our hearts from troubles and fears. Let us remember, too, that He loved His disciples to the end, despite their doubts and imperfections. And let us do our best to follow His example."

As Reverend Andrews left the pulpit and the organist struck up the introduction for "Amazing Grace," the congregation stood. Sam's sleeve brushed against her arm, and Cara wondered if he had been as moved by the minister's sermon as she had been. On the pretense of checking the hymn number on the board near the front, she risked a sideways peek at him. He was focused on the sanctuary, a slight frown marring his brow. Then, as if sensing her discreet perusal, he suddenly angled his head toward her.

Caught staring, she tried to avert her face as warmth crept up her neck. But his expression stopped her. An expression that was equal parts contrition, regret and yearning, compelling in its depth and intensity. There was almost a pleading in it, an entreaty, as clear as if he'd said the words. *I'm sorry for everything. Please give me another chance.*

Cara didn't know how to respond. Once upon a time, she and Sam had had the ingredients for the kind of marriage Reverend Andrews had held up as an example. But along the way, some of them had gone bad. And the marriage had fallen flat, like a soufflé that deflates when exposed to a sudden chill.

That had always been one of Cara's great sorrows. To her, marriage was forever. Till death do us part, according to the vows she and Sam had recited the day they were wed. That's why she'd never sought a divorce.

But she wasn't sure their marriage was salvageable. Despite Sam's actions, which had suggested in nonverbal ways that he'd like a chance to make amends and try again, and despite the Lord's call to love, to trust, to forgive, there were a couple of major problems.

She wasn't sure she could forgive Sam's betrayal. Nor could she seem to get past her fear. She'd trusted once and been betrayed. How could she be sure it wouldn't happen again?

Somehow, in the crush of people leaving the church after services, Marge managed to edge through the crowd and join Sam and Cara as they inched toward the door.

"You two are coming for coffee, aren't you?"

"I am," Cara responded.

"Dr. Martin? You'll come, too, won't you? Of course you will." Without giving him a chance to decline, she shouldered her way between them and linked her arms with theirs, as if to ensure that neither could escape. "Have you been thinking about the restaurant idea, Cara?"

Aware that Sam was once again looking at her, Cara shifted her purse higher on her shoulder and kept her focus on Marge. "Yes. I was going to talk to you about it today. I'll be happy to help for as long as I'm here."

"Hallelujah! I was praying in church this morning that you'd sign on. Looks like God was listening." Turning to Sam, Marge smiled. "Won't this be a boon for Oak Hill? Imagine…a restaurant started by a Cordon Bleu chef!"

At Sam's puzzled look, Cara spoke up. "I…uh…didn't get a chance to tell Sam about the idea, Marge."

"Goodness, I hope I didn't let the cat out of the bag!" The woman gave her a dismayed look, then shrugged. "But everyone in town will know about it soon, anyway." She proceeded to fill Sam in on the plan as they walked.

She finished as they stepped into the hall, and several ladies made a beeline for them.

"Oh, that's the kitchen committee for the Fourth of July booth," Marge explained to Cara. "They have a few questions. Let me introduce you."

As Cara did her best to focus on the women's questions, she heard Sam ask a question of his own, and out of the corner of her eye she watched Marge draw him off to one side. Although she couldn't hear their conversation, she could see Marge's animation and the speculative glances Sam directed her way. A short while later, she saw Reverend Andrews stop by to greet Sam, and long after Marge had flitted off, the minister and Sam continued to talk, a bit apart from the crowd, their expressions intent and serious.

Not until they were headed out to the car twenty minutes later did Cara have a chance to speak to Sam again. And she wasn't quite sure what to say. For some reason, she felt a need to explain her reticence about her two projects with Marge. But she wasn't even sure how to explain it to herself. She'd had ample opportunity to share the news with Sam over dinner the past couple of days. Why hadn't she? She'd certainly had no hesitation about discussing it with Liz, or seeking her friend's advice.

"Marge told me you've upgraded the menu for the church booth at the Fourth of July festival." Sam broke the uncomfortable silence between them as they wove through the cars in the parking lot, his tone casual and conversational.

"She more or less roped me into it."

"That sounds like Marge." He opened her door, waited until she slid in, closed it. A few seconds later he took his place behind the wheel and inserted his key in the ignition. "The restaurant sounds interesting, too."

Fiddling with her seat belt gave Cara an excuse to avert her face. "I probably should have mentioned it, but I only decided last night to get involved."

"You don't owe me any explanations, Cara."

While there was no recrimination in his voice, she felt guilty nonetheless. They were sharing the same roof, after all. And they ate dinner together every night—at her suggestion. Not to mention that he'd been there for her when she'd had the panic attack. Cara sighed as she secured her seat belt. This arrangement wasn't turning out to be as simple as she'd hoped. There weren't supposed to be any obligations.

Feeling the need to respond to his comment, Cara tried to downplay her involvement. "It's not a big deal, anyway. Marge thinks she can get this up and running before I leave, but I doubt that will happen. I'm just going to help with the start-up plans."

"I'm sure you'll do a great job. And as a veteran of Gus's, I can guarantee it will be a success. Oak Hill is in desperate need of a fine dining option." He turned onto his street. "I have to run into Rolla to visit a hospitalized patient. I'll drop you off by the back door, if that's okay. Shall I bring back some Chinese food for dinner?"

Grateful that he'd changed the subject, Cara endorsed his idea. She'd planned to roast a pork tenderloin, but it would keep until tomorrow. Then she fell silent again and stared out the window. Sitting beside Sam in church had brought back memories of happier times. And the look he'd given her after the sermon—the one that told her he wanted a second chance—had been unnerving.

What unnerved her even more, however, was that she was beginning to feel the same way Sam did. But starting over would require her to forgive. And she'd have to learn to trust again. Two tasks that seemed impossible.

Opening her door the instant he came to a stop, she scrambled out of the car, anxious to put some distance between them. But as Sam drove off, Cara knew that physical distance wasn't going to keep her safe. Sam seemed to be on a quest to prove that he was a changed man, and despite her best defenses, he was making inroads on her heart.

The church booth at the Fourth of July festival was a resounding success.

With a satisfied smile, Cara pushed a few damp tendrils of hair off her forehead and surveyed the long lines. Despite the high humidity and near-hundred-degree weather, they'd done a steady business since opening three hours ago. At this rate, they'd be sold out before the official seven o'clock closing, an hour away—putting to rest any lingering skepticism from the church ladies about whether the locals would embrace the new menu.

"Sorry I was gone so long, but my copier is slow as molasses." Marge appeared at Cara's elbow, puffing as she fanned herself with the sheaf of papers in her hand. Pulling a handkerchief out of the pocket of her red, white and blue shirt, which was adorned with sequined appliqués of the U.S. flag, the Statue of Liberty and George Washington, she wiped her brow. "Typical Fourth of July in Missouri. You could fry an egg on the sidewalk."

Tucking the square of limp linen back into her pocket, she plopped the papers on the edge of the food booth.

"You don't waste any time, do you?" Cara picked up one of the flyers, which advised customers that if they had enjoyed their Fourth of July dinner, they should call the Oak Hill Inn and inquire about the soon-to-open restaurant.

"He who hesitates is lost. But even I didn't expect all the flyers to disappear before we closed. I told you the idea would be a hit. Especially after folks taste the great menu you put together for today."

"I agree."

At the sound of Sam's voice, both women turned. He was juggling a plate of food in one hand and a cone of cotton candy in the other.

"Now that's an interesting combination," Marge pronounced.

"This is for me." Sam lifted the plate. "And this—" he indicated the cotton candy "—is for Cara. If she can take a break."

"Of course she can take a break," Marge declared. "She's been working like a dog for the past two days, and she's been on her feet in this heat since we set up at one o'clock. Go, find a shady spot and sit. Enjoy the band concert. We'll close things up here. You've done more than your share." She waved them off.

"I guess I have my instructions." Cara flexed the muscles in her shoulders. "And I don't think I'm going to argue. I'm used to the heat in kitchens, but the humidity here is pretty draining."

As she spoke, a family vacated a bench not far from the bandstand in the center of the town park, and Sam headed that direction. "Let's claim that spot before someone beats us to it."

Once seated, he held out the cotton candy. "I figured

you'd already eaten dinner. Or sampled enough at the booth to count as dinner. This is dessert."

Touched by the gesture, Cara reached for the cone of pink spun sugar. Despite her Cordon Bleu credentials, she'd always had a weakness for this treat, which evoked memories of her childhood, of country fairs and school picnics and trips to the circus with her family, when her dad had bought her and her sister cotton candy. She'd mentioned that to Sam once, early in their relationship. After that, whenever they went somewhere that offered carnival fare, he'd buy her a cone. But it had been years since he'd done so. She'd assumed he'd forgotten.

If she was surprised by his thoughtfulness, she was even more surprised that he'd come to the festival. Marge had told her that he hadn't appeared at any of the community events since moving to town. He'd said nothing to Cara about attending, so she'd figured he would spend the day working, as he had most of the holidays during their marriage.

Of course, she'd been guilty of that, too. There was no such thing as a day off in the restaurant business. Holidays simply meant more work. While Cara had drawn the line at Christmas and Easter, reserving those days for God, Sam had always been at the hospital. Holidays had come and gone for them as a couple with almost no notice. That he was here today was yet more evidence that he'd changed.

"Marge is really excited about this restaurant idea, isn't she?" Sam interrupted her musings as he dug into his plate of food.

"Yes. She's even convinced Abby Warner to do a feature story on it in the *Gazette*." She pulled off a tuft of cotton candy and popped it in her mouth, smiling as it dissolved into sweetness on her tongue. "Mmm. I haven't had this in years."

An answering smile played at Sam's lips. "I always loved that little-girl look you get on your face when you eat it."

Suddenly self-conscious, Cara dipped her head and steered the conversation in a different direction. "How come you're not working today? You always did rounds, or handled emergencies or caught up on paperwork on holidays."

"Family practice is a whole different ball game. Since I never have more than a patient or two hospitalized at once, it doesn't take long to do rounds. I manage to handle paperwork during normal working hours. And Stella, my receptionist, is a whiz at all the insurance forms. I do handle emergencies if they come up, but most of them can be dealt with by phone. It's a different life here, Cara."

And what about the old one, Sam? Do you still miss it as desperately as you once did? Or have you truly made peace with what happened?

The questions whirled around in her mind as Cara plucked at her cotton candy, but she left them unspoken. If she wanted to keep things impersonal, those were topics best left untouched.

They continued to eat in silence, watching as the local band began assembling in the gazebo for the concert. Families were gathering in groups, some in lawn chairs, others on blankets that had been spread on the ground. Children scampered about, and laughter rang in the air. It was small-town America at its best.

As Cara finished her cotton candy, Sam devoured the last of his dinner, chasing one elusive piece of pasta around on his plate with his plastic fork until he managed to spear it.

Cara couldn't help smiling. "You must have liked it."

"I'd go back for seconds, but I'm too late." He gestured toward the food booth, where Marge was posting a Sold Out sign. "Shall I get rid of that for you?" He reached for the empty paper cone.

"It's pretty sticky."

"That's okay."

Acquiescing, she handed it over.

"Sit tight. I don't want to lose our spot for the concert."

"You're staying?" Surprise lifted her eyebrows.

"I hear it's the thing to do on the Fourth of July. And there will be fireworks in the ball field outside of town after dark."

Before she could respond, he headed toward a trash can near the food booth.

In all the years they'd been together, she and Sam had attended a mere handful of concerts together. And they'd never watched a fireworks display, she realized. Work had always intruded. Perhaps tonight would give her a taste of what it might have been like had they made a success of their marriage.

"You were right, it was sticky." Sam rejoined her on the bench, wiping his hands on a damp paper napkin. When he finished, he turned to her, grinning. "And I'm not the only one with a souvenir. Someone has a cotton candy mustache."

Embarrassed, Cara scrubbed at her upper lip with her fingers. But she went still when Sam touched her hand. "Let me."

For an instant, neither moved. Cara knew she could resist his gentle tug on her hand. Knew she *should* resist. But the look in Sam's eyes melted her resolve. She let him remove her hand, then stopped breathing as he dabbed at her upper lip, leaning close enough that his breath fanned her cheeks. Close enough for her to drown in the depths of his deep blue eyes. Close enough to remember what it had been like to feel his strong arms close around her as she lost herself in his kiss.

As Sam stared at the woman he loved, a whisper away, and saw the sudden yearning in her eyes, his mouth went dry and his hand hesitated for a heartbeat. He'd never been good at reading the subtleties of expression, but he knew every nuance of his wife's features. The look on her unguarded face now, soft and filled with invitation, reminded him of the way she had always looked during their most tender moments. Welcoming and receptive to his touch. Sending him a silent plea to show her how much he cared.

His gaze dropped to her soft lips, and for a brief second he was tempted to claim them, to forget all that had gone before and forge a new beginning. Tempted enough to lean toward her—only to be jolted back to common sense by the ringing of his cell phone.

The spell broken, Cara backed off as quickly as a squirrel scuttling up a tree. Sam balled the damp napkin in his fist as he reached for his phone.

He kept the conversation brief, afraid if he talked too long she'd slip away, his attention fixed on her. The late-afternoon sun cast a golden glow on her profile, drawing out the fiery highlights in her hair and sparking the tips of her long lashes. She moistened her lips, whether from nervousness or to catch a lingering fleck of sticky sweetness from the cotton candy he wasn't sure. Not that it mattered. The innocent gesture drew his attention to her lips again… and that led back to memories of their kisses…and all at once he lost track of the conversation he was having.

Forcing himself to refocus, he completed the call and flipped the phone shut, trying to stifle his disappointment. "I've got an emergency. I need to see a patient in Rolla." His voice came out more husky than usual.

"No problem."

He hesitated, reluctant to end this interlude, and didn't attempt to hide his regret when he rose at last. "I doubt I'll finish in time to catch any of the concert. But I'll try to make it back for the fireworks. Will you be okay by yourself?"

"I'm fine, Sam. Don't hurry on my account."

She lifted her face, exposing the delicate column of her throat. Once more, an overpowering urge to kiss her swept over him. It took every ounce of his willpower to force himself to turn away.

As he strode toward his car, determined to handle this emergency with record speed, he replayed her parting words.

Don't hurry back on my account.

And he wouldn't.

He was planning to hurry back on *his* account.

* * *

From her seat on the porch swing, Cara had a clear view of the fireworks being shot off from the ball field on the edge of town. It was a fine display, and she was enjoying it. But she wished Sam had arrived back in time to watch it with her.

And that wasn't a good thing.

In fact, she wasn't sure her whole visit was a good thing.

There had been some benefits, of course. Memories of the shooting were losing their power to freak her out. She'd only had one panic attack since arriving. And her nightmares had ceased.

But her long-buried feelings for Sam were resurfacing with an intensity that alarmed her. She'd been certain they had died. Obviously she'd been wrong. They were still there, deep inside. Waiting to be reignited. And Sam's transformation had been the flint that sparked them back to life.

From the day she'd left him, Cara had known that Sam regretted all he'd done to alienate her. In the first months of their separation, he'd written notes, left messages on her answering machine, sent flowers. She'd never read the letters. And she had erased the messages without listening to them, given the flowers to an elderly neighbor. Yet she'd recognized the gestures as his attempt to apologize. Except her heart hadn't been open to forgiveness, let alone reconciliation. She'd been hurting too much.

But Reverend Andrews's sermon had been replaying in her mind ever since Sunday. God did call His people to love. To forgive. To put fear aside, and to trust. Had Cara come to Oak Hill and found the Sam she'd left— arrogant, angry, bitter—those instructions would have been difficult, if not impossible, to follow.

Instead, she'd discovered a changed man. A man who was doing everything possible to express his contrition and caring. A man who was struggling to build a new life, humbled by the suffering he'd endured. A man who wanted to fit in but wasn't quite sure how to go about it. A man who was doing the best he could.

In other words, a man of courage and compassion and integrity.

The kind of man she could fall in love with all over again.

And therein lay the problem.

The sudden sound of a car turning into the driveway drew her attention, and a second later headlights swept the front of the detached garage.

He was back.

As she debated whether to scurry into the house, the decision was taken out of her hands. Sam strode down the path, stopping when he saw her on the porch swing.

"You didn't go the fireworks."

"I figured I could see them just as well from here and I wouldn't have to worry about the crowd."

Sam wasn't surprised she'd come back to the house, knowing how skittish she was about being out at night alone. That was one of the reasons he'd driven as fast as he dared on the narrow country roads, hoping to arrive home in time to take her to the display. But from miles away he'd seen the glow in the sky and realized he'd never make it in time. Finding her on the back porch was a bonus.

The other reason he'd pushed the speed limit was because he wanted to share the fireworks experience with her. And it might not be too late for that, he realized, his spirits rising.

"Is that seat taken?" He gestured toward the other side of the porch swing.

"No." The night hid her expression, but he noticed that she scooted over as far as the seat would allow. At least she didn't go inside.

Settling down beside her, he set the swing swaying with a gentle push. As he propped one elbow on the back, careful to avoid brushing her shoulder, he noted that Cara had folded her arms across her chest.

"Good display." It had been a long time since he'd watched fireworks. And never with his wife. He hoped this might be the beginning of a new tradition.

"Yes."

They swung in silence for a couple of minutes, the boom of the fireworks a distant rumble in the quiet air.

"Did you stay for the band concert?"

"Some of it."

"How did you get home?"

"Marge dropped me off. Everything okay in Rolla?"

"Mmm-hmm." It was a simple, end-of-the-day conversation. The kind long-married folks might have. The kind he wanted back in his life.

All at once the sky burst into a kaleidoscope of brilliant color as multiple fireworks exploded for the finale.

It was stunning—but too brief. In less than twenty seconds, it was all over.

"I guess I'll call it a night." Cara eased off the swing as the last bits of color faded from the sky. "See you tomorrow."

She slipped through the back door without waiting for him to respond.

For another ten minutes, Sam stayed on the porch swing, gently rocking. The sky grew dark again, the brief dazzle of the fireworks already but a memory. Like his marriage.

His life before Cara had been like the night sky, he reflected. Then she'd given him her love, illuminating his world just as the finale had illuminated the heavens. And when she'd gone, the darkness had somehow seemed blacker than before, just as the night sky did now, bereft of the glittering fireworks.

With each day that passed, his determination to win her back strengthened. He couldn't let her walk away again, taking the light with her and leaving him in darkness. He wouldn't survive it.

Closing his eyes, he turned to prayer, as he had been doing more and more often in recent days.

Lord, please soften Cara's heart toward me. I have a feeling she's beginning to recognize that I've changed. I ask that You help that process along. And when—or if—she can acknowledge that, then I ask my biggest favor of all. Help her find the compassion to forgive me so we can have a second chance at love.

Chapter Ten

"Goodness, you'd think people in this town hadn't had a decent meal in years the way the reservations are pouring in for the opening." Marge bustled into the kitchen at the inn, waving a slip of paper. "Not that I'm complaining, you understand. The response just validates what I said all along. But the Fourth of July was what…five days ago?…and we're booked solid for the whole opening weekend. Those flyers did the trick."

"Let's just hope we can pull it all together by then. We only have two weeks." Cara double-checked the supplies that had been delivered that morning as she responded to Marge.

"I'm not worried in the least." Marge shook out a linen napkin from the stack on the kitchen table and began to fold it into a rosette.

"That makes one of us."

"My dear, if I've learned one lesson in life, it's this. Never let fear keep you from seizing every opportunity.

That's how I became an innkeeper. And look how well that turned out."

"I've been wondering how you ended up in Oak Hill." Cara paused in her methodical inventory and turned to the older woman. In typical Marge style, she wore a pair of hot-pink Capri pants and a psychedelic-patterned top in shades of pink, orange and lime-green, with a dollop of royal-purple thrown in for good measure. It was cinched at the waist with a heavy, silver-link belt studded with an array of flashy rhinestones.

"It's quite a story, but—" Marge surveyed the pile of napkins on the table "—I expect we have a few minutes while I work my way through this mountain." She picked up another square of linen and proceeded to crease it into precise folds. "It all started eight years ago. My husband, Stan, and I had a nice life in Boston. He was an accountant, and I taught kindergarten. My, how I loved those youngsters. Stan and I never had children of our own, but my little ones in school helped ease that disappointment.

"Life was good until Stan up and died on me. Heart attack. By the time I got to the hospital, he was almost gone. He only had time to say six words. 'I love you, Marge. I'm sorry.'" She cleared her throat and continued to fold. "It was quite a shock, I must say. The second biggest one of my life."

"The second biggest?" Cara ventured.

Selecting another napkin, Marge nodded. "The biggest one came after Stan died, when I figured out what his deathbed apology was all about. Turns out he was a compulsive gambler. Had been for twenty years. I'd always trusted him to handle the finances, so I had no idea we were hocked to the hilt when he died. Took every penny I could scrounge up—and then some—to pay off the debts."

Stunned, Cara stared at the affable innkeeper. Her husband had betrayed her, as surely as Sam had betrayed Cara—in intent, if not in deed.

"You think you know a man, but..." Marge shrugged. "We all have our secrets, I guess. And Stan was perfect for me in every other way. I did a lot of research about gambling after he died, trying to understand what drove him. Came to find out it's an addiction. Like alcohol or drugs.

"Anyway, not long after Stan passed, my aunt here in Oak Hill died. She'd never had any children, either, and she left me this place. I looked into selling it, but there wasn't much of a market for a pink elephant. So I prayed about it, and after a while I figured maybe the Lord was offering me an opportunity to start over. I had enough years in at my job to retire, and I was going to lose the house Stan and I had lived in anyway because of the home equity loans he'd taken against it. Long story short, that's how I ended up as an Oak Hill innkeeper."

Marge continued folding napkins while Cara processed her startling disclosure—and tried to figure out how to discreetly ask the questions zipping through her mind.

As if sensing her dilemma, Marge gave her a smile. "Ask away, my dear. I can see the question marks all over your face. I trust your discretion or I wouldn't be in business with you."

A faint hint of color tinged Cara's cheeks. "I don't want to be nosy."

"Nosy." Marge gave an unladylike snort. "Honey, it isn't being nosy when someone gives you permission to ask questions. What would you like to know?"

"I guess I'm trying to figure out why you don't feel any resentment toward your husband. You trusted him to handle your finances, and he betrayed you."

"Now don't go painting me as a saint, Cara." She shook out a napkin with a bit more force than necessary. "Of course I was angry at first. That's only natural. When someone you have faith in violates your trust, it's a shock. You feel deceived. And hurt. But I knew that Stan was a good man at heart. And the fact is, circumstances can often drive people to behave in uncharacteristic ways."

She picked up another napkin. "From what I could determine, his gambling didn't reach the out-of-control stage until the year before he died—when he got a new boss who was making his life miserable. Stan never told me that, but I found out about it from his coworkers after he died. I suspect the excessive gambling was his way of coping with the pressure at work. It was a release valve for him. Not a healthy one, of course. But stress can drive people to do things they later regret."

Cara folded her arms across her chest and leaned against the counter. "I admire your ability to overlook that kind of deception and maintain such a positive attitude."

"I'm not excusing Stan, Cara." Marge stopped folding and faced the younger woman, her usual light-hearted demeanor absent for once. "But after a lot of research and a lot of prayer, I came to understand what drove him. That understanding helped me forgive. That, and the certainty that Stan felt remorse for what he'd done—and never stopped loving me. Bottom line, he was a good man who made mistakes. As we all do. If love was contingent on perfection, this world would be a pretty lonely place."

It was hard to argue with Marge's reasoning, Cara admitted. The little kitchen philosophy lesson rang true. And it was consistent with Reverend Andrews's sermon. Love should be unqualified. And because people weren't perfect, forgiveness had to be part of it.

In theory, Cara accepted all of that. Putting it into practice was another story, however. That took courage and faith and a willingness to trust, even after trust has been compromised. She wasn't sure she was up to the task.

"I appreciate your sharing all that with me, Marge."

The innkeeper added another folded napkin to the long row on the table. "No sense keeping it a secret if there's a chance it might help someone else." Without giving Cara a chance to respond, Marge inclined her head toward the dining room. "What do you say we play around with the table arrangement a bit?"

"Sure."

As Cara followed Marge into the inn's dining room, she added two more sterling qualities to the list of attributes that the gregarious innkeeper possessed.

Insight and generosity.

And she prayed that the Lord would help her find the strength to emulate them. Especially when it came to forgiving Sam.

* * *

"Cara? Sam. I hate to bother you, but I could use a favor, if you have a few minutes."

Since the Fourth of July nine days ago, Sam had been calling Cara at least once a day with some sort of question. Could he pick up anything in Rolla for her while he was there? Would she like him to swing by at lunchtime with an ice-cream sundae from the soda fountain on Main Street? Would she mind sharing that recipe for beef burgundy with the patient he'd seen that morning, who'd asked for it after Sam had raved about the dish? It was almost as if he was searching for excuses to talk with her. But this was the first time he'd asked a favor.

Surprised, Cara checked her watch. She'd planned to run into town and drop off some menu ideas with Marge, but there was no rush. It was Saturday afternoon, and the innkeeper had said that most of her guests were out sightseeing. She was available anytime. "Sure. What do you need?"

"I'm on my way back from Rolla, and I just had a call from the sheriff. His daughter fell off her bike and cut her chin. He's meeting me at the office. I know she's allergic to a couple of things, and I'd feel better if I had her chart in front of me when I treat her. But I brought it home last week to finish some notes after I saw her for a virus, and I think it's still on my desk."

"It's Jenna Lewis, isn't it?"

"Yes. How did you know?"

"I met them at church. Hang on and I'll check."

It wasn't hard to find the chart in Sam's tidy home

office. A couple of minutes later, she was back on the phone. "Got it."

"Great. Now here's the real favor. Is there any chance you could bring it by the office? It would save me a few minutes."

"No problem. I was going into town anyway."

"Thanks. I'll see you there."

His clipped, professional tone was familiar to Cara, but it was the first time she'd heard him use it since her arrival in Oak Hill. It was how Sam always sounded when he was concentrating on a medical issue. In some ways, it was reassuring to know that he'd been able to hold on to that little piece of his past. His singular focus and thoroughness had been legendary, and those qualities seemed to have translated to his new specialty.

Ten minutes later, when Cara pulled up in front of his office, she found the sheriff and his tearful young daughter waiting.

"Hello, Sheriff," she greeted him when she drew close. "Sam left Jenna's chart at home and he asked me to bring it by."

"Sorry to put you out. But I think this needs immediate attention."

"It's always better to err on the side of caution." Cara transferred her attention to the little girl who was clutching Dale's leg. Her ponytail had slipped, and a large, lopsided piece of gauze had been taped to her chin.

As she took in the tear tracks down the youngster's cheek, a rush of tenderness washed over Cara. Children had always held a special place in her heart. Often, during the past couple of years, she'd wondered if a child would have helped her and Sam refocus their priorities on family and each other. But she'd heard that instead of shoring up a flagging marriage, a child served only to magnify the stress.

Besides, pregnancy had always eluded them, despite a battery of tests that had revealed nothing amiss. When at last they'd given up hope, Cara had begun to consider adoption. But by then, Sam had lost interest. His schedule was already packed and he'd told her he didn't see how he could squeeze in the duties of fatherhood.

Cara hadn't pushed the issue. And eventually, she'd come to believe that they weren't meant to have children.

But all it took was an encounter with a youngster like this to remind her how much she'd always wanted a family.

Pushing aside her regrets, she dropped down to the little girl's level and forced her lips into a smile.

"Hi, Jenna. It looks like you had an accident."

"I f-falled off my bike. D-Daddy says I might need st-stitches."

"That happened to me once, too. Except I cut my forehead. I had to get six stitches. If you look real close, you can still see a tiny white scar." She moved her hair aside and pointed to a spot near her scalp.

Curious, the little girl edged closer. "D-did it hurt when you got the stitches?"

"Not very much. And Dr. Martin will be very careful. He tries hard not to hurt people. Besides, you're a big girl. I bet you're very brave. How old are you?"

"Four." As they spoke, Jenna's grip on Dale's leg eased. "You have pretty hair."

"I'm glad you like it. When I was little, all the kids

teased me. They said it was the color of a fire truck, and whenever they saw me they made a sound like a siren." The little girl's unexpected giggle warmed Cara's heart. "I always wanted blond hair like yours."

"Daddy says my mommy had blond hair."

At Jenna's wistful expression, Cara recalled Marge's running commentary as she'd introduced congregants during that first coffee hour. Dale was a widower, the innkeeper had said.

She was saved from having to reply by Sam's arrival. When he emerged from the car, the little girl once more tightened her grip on her father's leg.

"It will be okay, honey," Cara soothed, brushing a few strands of Jenna's silky hair back from her cheek.

"Sorry to keep you waiting." Sam addressed his comment to the group, then dropped down beside Cara and spoke with the little girl. "Hi, Jenna. Did you fall off your bike?"

"Y-yes."

"How about if we go into my office and take a look?"

"W-will it hurt?"

"It might hurt a little bit, but not for very long."

Tears welled in her eyes again as Jenna turned to Cara. "Could you stay with me?"

Taken aback, Cara looked from Jenna to Sam. She'd planned to hand him the chart and head out. But it was hard to resist the little girl's plea.

"If you have the time, it might help calm her," Sam said.

Rising, Cara kept one hand on Jenna's shoulder as she spoke to Dale. "Is that all right with you?"

"I'd appreciate it very much. Dads are great, but

nothing replaces a woman's touch." A brief spark of pain flared in his eyes, come and gone as quickly as the fireworks on the Fourth of July.

"I'm happy to do it." Cara reached for Jenna's hand and smiled at the youngster. "Let's go with Dr. Martin and see what he thinks."

As they crossed the waiting room, Cara noted that the space appeared to have undergone a recent update. It was modern but impersonal, and she was left with an impression of quiet but sterile elegance.

The inner office consisted of a reception area, two examining rooms and Sam's office. Sam led the way to the second examining room, and Dale lifted Jenna onto the table. Sam washed his hands and withdrew a few supplies, then began to peel off the bandage in silence.

When Jenna's sudden whimper echoed in the quiet room, Cara decided diversionary tactics were in order. She tried sending a silent message to Sam, but since he was focused on Jenna's injury she stepped in.

"Do you go to school, Jenna?"

The youngster sniffled. "Just preschool. In the morning."

"I bet you meet a lot of nice boys and girls there."

"Y-yes. Leah's my best friend. She has a dog."

While Cara engaged Jenna in conversation, she watched Sam's progress out of the corner of her eye. After the bandage was off, he cleaned around the gash, his touch gentle. Jenna winced once or twice, but Sam paused while Cara once more engaged her in conversation, waiting until the child was distracted again before resuming.

When he straightened, Dale stepped close. "What do you think?"

"It's not as bad as it looks," Sam replied. "It's long, but only the center part is deep. I think three stitches will take care of it. It shouldn't leave much of a scar, if any."

"That's good news." Relief flooded Dale's features. Then his gaze dropped for a brief second to Sam's right hand. "Can you do it here, or do I need to take her to Rolla?"

A humorless smile twisted Sam's lips. "I think I can handle it. I used to be a surgeon."

He angled away, and Cara saw the flicker of surprise on the sheriff's face, suggesting that Sam had never shared his past with his patients. Dale's next words confirmed that.

"I'm sorry. I didn't know that."

When Sam turned back, his face was more composed. "No problem. I don't talk about it much. Okay, Jenna, this won't take long at all. Can you lie back for me, and turn your head a little bit so I can see your chin?"

"Your daddy and I will be right here," Cara assured her as she eased the little girl back.

Dale moved beside his daughter and took her hand, while Cara stroked her forehead. As Cara eyed the needle for the local anesthetic, which Sam kept discreetly out of sight, she sent him a look. Catching her glance this time, he raised an eyebrow in query.

"Maybe you could talk about what you're doing while you're working. That way, we'll all know what's going on," Cara suggested in a conversational tone.

It was only the second time in their relationship that

Cara had offered professional advice to Sam. But at the farmhouse, it had worked. And Sam's response indicated he remembered that, too.

"By the way, Marv Jackson's doing a lot better."

A smile hovered at the corners of Cara's lips. "I'm glad."

"Okay, Jenna." Sam turned his attention to his patient and smiled. "Before I sew up that nasty little cut, I'm going to numb your chin so you won't feel anything when I work on it."

"Like when I sit on my leg and it goes to sleep?"

"That's right. But first I have to give you a couple of quick little pricks to put the skin to sleep, okay? Hold on to your daddy's hand, and I'll do this real fast."

Following Cara's lead, Sam talked Jenna through the process, leaving Cara free to observe his technique. In all their years of marriage, she'd never seen Sam work. Operating rooms were off-limits to nonessential personnel. While today's procedure hardly qualified as major surgery, it did give her some insight into his skills. He worked with deft, sure strokes, compensating for his disability with amazing proficiency—and giving Cara a hint of the lifesaving talent Sam had once possessed in his hands.

True to his promise, Sam finished in a matter of minutes. As he sent Cara and Jenna to search the drawers in his receptionist's desk for her stash of lollipops, Dale watched them disappear down the hallway.

"Cara has a real knack with kids," he commented while Sam washed up.

"Yes. She does." He hadn't seen her with children

very often, and he, too, had been struck by her ability to make an instant connection with Jenna. While he'd been too wrapped up in his career to let their inability to produce an offspring cause him much distress, the soft light in Cara's eyes as she interacted with his young patient had given him a glimmer of what a great sadness and disappointment it had been for her.

"Listen, I'm sorry about my earlier question. You did a great job with Jenna."

Turning back to Dale, Sam wiped his hands on a towel. "No problem. Considering how this looks—" he extended his scarred hand "—I expect I'd have had the same concerns if our situations were reversed. I'll never do surgery again, but I can manage simpler procedures."

For a long moment Dale studied him. When he spoke, his voice was quiet and sincere. "I don't know what caused that—" he nodded toward Sam's hand "—but I do know that the people of Oak Hill are glad you're here. It's not easy to attract good doctors to small towns. We feel lucky to have you." He extended his hand, and Sam took it in a firm grip, surprised by the unexpected emotion that clogged his throat at the sheriff's heartfelt words.

"I picked a purple one, Daddy!" Jenna interrupted, holding up a lollipop. All trace of her fear had vanished.

"That looks good. Say thank you to Dr. Martin."

The little girl gave him a shy look as she complied.

Dropping down to her level once again, Sam smiled. "No more falling off bikes, okay? We don't want to do this again, do we?" She shook her head, and he rose to speak with Dale. "Bring her back in five or six days. In the meantime, change the bandage every day and put some of this cream on the cut." He handed over a sample packet.

"Will do. Thanks again for meeting us on a Saturday."

"That's why I'm here."

Turning to Cara, Dale held out his hand. "Thank you, too. Your presence made a big difference."

"I'm glad I could help."

As they watched the father and daughter leave, Sam folded his arms across his chest as he regarded his wife. "This seems to be a day for saying thank you."

"I was coming to town anyway. I didn't mind dropping off the chart. Or staying with Jenna." She picked up her purse, preparing to leave.

"I was referring more to the lesson in patient relations."

His gratitude took her off guard, and she lifted one shoulder in a dismissive gesture, fiddling with her purse strap. "Medicine is routine for doctors, but it's a mysterious thing for most patients. I think it helps subdue fears when doctors explain what's being done, and why—whether the patient is a child *or* an adult."

"I'll remember that."

Searching his face, Cara looked for some hint of sarcasm or arrogance but found none. "I wasn't sure you'd be receptive to my suggestion," she ventured.

That didn't surprise Sam. He was well aware of the egotism and self-importance he'd exhibited in his old life. The hard truth was that while he may have excelled at surgery, he'd become less and less likable as the years went by. In the end, he'd had colleagues but few friends. He'd even alienated his wife with his conceit and pride.

Then had come his fall.

Dealing with his disintegrating marriage and career had been the most horrendous experience of his life. Yet good had come out of it, he acknowledged. He'd been forced to take a long, hard look at himself—and he hadn't liked what he'd seen. If nothing else, he'd learned that he didn't have all the answers. That he was as vulnerable to loss and uncertainty and insecurity as the next person. It had been a humbling experience.

And since coming to Oak Hill, he'd learned something else as well. He might have been a great surgeon, but he hadn't been the best doctor. Doctors should treat the whole patient, not just the problem area. While he understood that principle at an intuitive level, he'd been struggling since his arrival in Oak Hill to put it into practice.

It had taken Cara's visit, and her subtle suggestions, for him to begin to understand why he wasn't as successful as he'd hoped. And to give him some much-needed direction about how to relate to his patients. He still had a long way to go, as today's experience with Jenna proved. But at least Cara had provided a map for him to follow.

Now, as she stood across from him in his office, he wanted to tell her how much her presence meant to him. That it comforted him and gave him hope that all could be made right in the end. But if relating to his patients was difficult, sharing what was in his heart was even more of a challenge. Especially when he knew that in trying to pull her close, he could just as easily push her away if she wasn't ready to listen. And since he wasn't all that confident about his timing, fear kept him silent.

Realizing that he hadn't responded to Cara's comment, Sam stuck his hands in his pockets and drew an unsteady breath. "In my former life, I wouldn't have been receptive to suggestions. But I've learned a thing or two in the past eighteen months. About humility and patience and priorities. And the importance of communication. I've got a ways to go on that one, but I'm working on it. Your visit has helped a lot."

Soft color suffused her cheeks, and she played with the strap of her purse. "I haven't done much."

"More than you know." His words hung in the air for a moment, then he changed the subject. "Did you say you're off to see Marge?"

"Yes." Relief eased her features. "Abby Warner is going to interview us for a feature story in the *Gazette*. After that, Marge and I are going to finalize our plans for opening night."

"Reserve a table for me, okay?"

"Sure. I'll see you later."

He watched her leave—though perhaps *escape* would be a better word, he mused. She had become uncomfortable when the conversation took a personal turn. He hadn't pushed today, but soon he'd have to be a bit more assertive. Time was running out.

And while he wasn't the most communicative guy around, he wasn't about to let her walk away without telling her what was in his heart.

"I think that should wrap things up. If I have any more questions as I write the article, I'll let you know."

Abby Warner closed her notebook and smiled at Cara and Marge as she tucked it in her tote bag.

"Thanks for giving us the coverage, Abby," Marge said.

"Hey, a new restaurant in Oak Hill is big news. Especially when a chef like Cara is involved." She rose and slung her bag over her shoulder.

"How's everything going at the *Gazette?*" Marge inquired as they walked the editor to the door of the inn.

Cara watched, curious, as a shadow passed across Abby's face, dimming the brightness in her eyes for a moment, much as a drifting cloud subdues the sunlight.

"We're hanging in."

"Glad to hear it. I'll be in touch in a couple of days about running an ad."

"Thanks, Marge. We can never have too much ad revenue." Abby turned to Cara and extended her hand. "Good luck with the restaurant. I know it will be a success."

"Thank you. I'm afraid I won't be here long enough to reap the fruits of our labors, but it's been fun helping Marge get things rolling."

"I'll be sure to send over some extra copies of the paper next week, when this runs."

"We'd appreciate that," Marge said. "Take care, now."

As Marge shut the door behind the editor, Cara gave the innkeeper a quizzical look. She liked the petite, serious woman who ran the local newspaper, but she'd picked up some troublesome vibes as they said their goodbyes.

"I don't mean to pry, but it sounds like Abby has some sort of problem at the paper," she ventured.

"She does. At least, I think she does," Marge amended. "Abby's been pretty closemouthed about it, but I get the feeling that the *Gazette* is facing some serious financial difficulties. It's hard these days for small businesses to compete with the big conglomerates. But the *Gazette* is a family business, started by Abby's great-grandfather, and she's determined to carry on that tradition. I hope she succeeds."

As Marge and Cara returned to the kitchen to put the finishing touches on their plans for the opening weekend, Cara considered Marge's comments. In the past couple of years—and the past few weeks, in particular—she'd been focused on her own problems to the exclusion of almost everything else.

But in recent days she'd been reminded that she wasn't the only one dealing with serious personal issues. Marge had faced her own trauma, Abby appeared to be in a battle to retain her family business, the widowed sheriff was struggling to raise his young daughter alone and Sam was fighting to rebuild a shattered life and career.

No one, it seemed, was immune from problems.

Feeling suddenly selfish for bending God's ear about only her issues, she sent a silent prayer heavenward on behalf of all of the Oak Hill residents who were in need of aid.

"How did it go with Marge today?" Sam cut into the sautéed chicken breast glazed with a lemon-butter sauce that Cara had prepared for Saturday dinner.

"Things are moving a lot faster than I expected. The extra tables, linens and place settings have already arrived. And she was excited about the sample menus I gave her today for the second and third weekends. She's taking out an ad in the *Gazette*, in addition to the article they're going to run, and plans to open next Thursday."

"Is that feasible?"

"I wouldn't have thought so, but she seems able to make things happen. I guess it's easier to cut through red tape in a small town."

Spearing a piece of broccoli, Sam smiled. "At least it is when Marge is in charge. So what did you think of my office?"

For a nanosecond, Cara's fork hesitated halfway to her mouth. If Sam hadn't been paying close attention, he would have missed that clue. And when she tucked a piece of hair behind her ear, his antennae went all the way up. She'd always done that when she was unsure about bringing up a sticky subject. Such as their relationship. Or adopting a child.

"It looks as if it's been redone in the recent past."

Her noncommittal reply wasn't lost on Sam. Seeking to put her at ease, he smiled and responded in a teasing tone. "That sounds like a diplomatic, discreet—and evasive—answer. It's definitely a far cry from the sophisticated setup I had in Philadelphia."

Cara frowned She'd never liked his high-tech, sleek surgical offices. Maybe they'd instilled confidence in his patients, but they'd left her cold. And she hadn't intended to imply that she was comparing his new office to his old one.

"I like this office better."

"But…"

"Did you have it redone when you came here?"

"Yes. I worked with an interior designer in Rolla. When I took over, the place was a 1940s time warp. It was like something out of…"

When he struggled to find an apt description, Cara supplied one. "Norman Rockwell?"

"Yes."

"Is that bad?"

Now it was his turn to frown. "It was very dated."

"But warm. And cozy. And comfortable. Right?"

"Are you suggesting I should have left it as it was?"

"Not at all. You aren't Doc Adams, and your office should reflect your style and personality. I think the designer did a good job overall of bringing it into the twenty-first century. But the waiting room is a bit cold and impersonal. People are always nervous when they visit a doctor. The more you can do to alleviate their tension, the better the chance that they'll relax and tell you what's really bothering them."

"What would you suggest?" Sam rested his elbows on the table and linked his fingers.

"You might consider putting some books and toys in one corner, for kids like Jenna. A couple of plants would help a lot, too. And adding a few lamps would soften the effect of the fluorescent lighting and provide a homey touch."

As usual, Cara's insight impressed him. She had a knack for knowing how to put others at ease, and he was sure that her ideas for the waiting room would achieve that goal.

But *he* was the main problem in that regard—not his decor. He couldn't seem to bond with his patients. Oh, he treated their symptoms and cured the illnesses they brought to him as best he could. But he knew he wasn't connecting at a deep enough level to inspire the kind of confidences that would allow him to treat the whole person, not just the problem that had brought them to the office that day.

At Sam's sudden discouraged expression, Cara's stomach clenched. She hadn't intended to sound negative, not when she knew he was trying his best.

"I'm sorry, Sam. I didn't mean to be critical. I think you've done a great job creating a life here."

Though her compliment warmed him, it didn't change the facts.

"I appreciate that, Cara. But sometimes I wonder if I'll ever be a good family doctor. I just can't seem to establish a rapport with my patients. They come in and give me a list of their symptoms, I ask the appropriate questions, and I send them home with a prescription or test order or referral. But I always feel as if some piece is missing."

Setting her fork beside her plate, Cara took a sip of water. "Maybe it's a matter of expanding your list of appropriate questions."

"What do you mean?" He gave her a perplexed look.

"Well, when someone comes in and says their stomach hurts, what do you ask?"

"The usual. Did they eat anything out of the ordinary, are they running a temperature, where's the pain, what kind of pain is it, do they have discomfort anywhere else…all the things that will help me pinpoint the source of their problem."

"Those are all good medical questions, I'm sure. But do you ever ask them about what's going on in their lives?"

"I try not to infringe on people's privacy."

"I agree that it's important not to overstep. But there's a difference between being nosy and showing compassion and concern. Just because people are a bit reticent at first doesn't mean they don't want to talk. They might need a bit of coaxing…to be assured that the interest is real and not the equivalent of the ubiquitous 'Have a nice day.'"

She leaned forward, intent. "Patients want to know doctors care about them as people, not just cases. That may not have been quite as important in surgery. But my opinion, for whatever it's worth, is that it's vital to your new specialty. I think the best family practitioners are sensitive to the mind as well as the body."

It was difficult to argue with Cara's advice. Yet he didn't seem able to put it into practice. Sam averted his head as he responded. "I'm not sure I'm capable of that."

In the instant before he turned away, Cara glimpsed his despair. She didn't want to care about this man who had wounded her deeply, yet she couldn't suppress the compassion that rose up inside her. No matter what had happened between them in the past, he was trying his best to build a better future for himself. How could she be less than encouraging?

"I think you're being too hard on yourself."

"Am I?" He turned back to her, his expression despondent. "You, better than anyone, know how I've always struggled with communication. If I couldn't relate to my own wife, how can I ever hope to relate to my patients?"

Glancing down, she toyed with her fork and spoke in a soft voice. "Our relationship wasn't a priority for you at the end, Sam. If it had been, you'd have found a way to communicate, to share, like you did early in our marriage. I think your practice here *is* a priority. If you want to succeed, you will. You're capable of communication, even if it isn't a natural skill for you. You did it with me, once."

The wistful quality in her voice took Cara by surprise. She hadn't meant for her reply to come out sounding melancholy, and she hoped Sam hadn't noticed. But a quick look confirmed he had. As did his next comment.

"I do recognize the importance of communication, Cara. And I have been working on it. I guess I'll need to work harder until I get it right."

His gaze held hers, and Cara suspected he wanted to say more. But she wasn't yet ready to deal with Sam's feelings about their relationship.

Forcing herself to look away, she picked up her fork and resumed eating, praying Sam would drop the subject for tonight. Relief coursed through her when he turned back to his food.

"Dinner is great, Cara."

"Thanks. It's one of the items on the menu I gave to Marge."

For the remainder of the meal, they engaged in small talk. Yet there was nothing small about the decision

Cara faced. Each day that she stayed in Oak Hill brought her closer to dealing with Sam's obvious wish to make amends and with her own growing feelings. Closer to dealing with the whole forgiveness and trust issue that Marge's story had mirrored.

Of course, she could always return to Philadelphia sooner than planned. She'd intended to stay another couple of weeks, but her trip had already accomplished much of its purpose. The trauma from the shooting was receding more each day. If she hadn't agreed to help Marge with the restaurant, she could return now.

Cara tried to feel annoyed by the obligation. But in the end, she couldn't fool herself. She was glad she had an excuse to stay.

As for *why* she felt that way—she didn't want to deal with that yet, though.

Chapter Eleven

"Your eye should be fine, Charlie, but it was a close call. Where were your safety goggles?" Sam reached for a sterile pad and began cleaning the gouge below the construction worker's eyebrow. Already the puffy skin around it was black-and-blue.

The man shifted in his seat on the examining table and stared at the wall in front of him as Sam worked. "I forgot to wear them."

"You can't afford to be careless with a jackhammer. If that chip of rock had been half an inch lower, you could have lost your sight in this eye."

"Yeah. I guess I got lucky."

Sam didn't have much patience with people who took risks with their bodies, and he almost issued another, sharper reprimand. Except some inflection in the man's tone stopped him. Sarcasm, mixed with despair.

Thinking back to his conversation with Cara a few days before, Sam wondered if this was one of those occasions when he was supposed to dig a little deeper. Uncertain, he decided to follow his gut.

After cleaning and treating the wound, he sat on the stool beside the counter and drew the man's chart toward him. But instead of jotting his usual notes, he laid his pen aside and looked up at the construction worker.

"How's everything else going, Charlie?"

Surprise flickered in the man's eyes, and his response was tentative. "Okay."

Not a good start, Sam concluded. But Cara had told him he might have to press a bit. And she hadn't said it would be easy. He flicked a quick glance at the man's personal data on the chart.

"How's Susan?"

"Busy. Her Web design business is really taking off. She loves it."

"Glad to hear it." Nothing wrong from his wife's end, as far as Sam could tell. He tried again. "And how are the kids?"

"Joel's getting ready to go to college. Megan's… she's okay, I guess." A shadow of distress darkened the man's features for a brief instant.

Bingo.

"Has she been having some problems?" Sam kept his tone conversational.

"I'm not sure." Charlie drew an unsteady breath and looked down at his work-roughened hands. "She's been hanging around with some kids I don't like. And at sixteen, peer pressure is tough to fight."

"That's true. This group of kids she's involved with… what is it you don't like about them?"

The man shrugged. "There are rumors that some of them are into drugs."

"Do you think Megan is using?" He recalled seeing the taciturn teen a couple of months ago for cold symptoms. Maybe the runny nose had been indicative of a far more serious problem, he mused.

"I don't know." Worry etched the man's features. "Susan and I have talked to her until we're blue in the face, but we can't seem to get through. She won't go see the counselor at school, and she says she's clean. But I just don't know…"

After a moment's consideration, Sam spoke. "I'll tell you what. Why don't you have her come see me? She hasn't had a physical since I've been here, and I should have some baseline information on record if I'm going to treat her. You can use that as an excuse to get her in here. I'll talk with her, see what I can find out."

The tightness in the man's features eased. "That would be great. I'll let Susan know, and one of us will call to make an appointment for Megan tomorrow."

"Good. In the meantime, take care of that eye. And remember the goggles."

The man gave a sheepish nod. "I will. I guess my mind's been on other things." He held out his hand and gave Sam's a firm shake. "Thanks again, Doctor. I appreciate your taking the time to talk with me."

As the man exited and Sam turned back to the counter to complete his notes, he realized that Cara had once again given him good advice. Had he not pushed a bit, he'd have attributed the accident to carelessness. Instead, worry had distracted Charlie, clouding his judgment. Their conversation had not only relieved his patient's mind, it may have uncovered another problem that needed to be addressed.

All thanks to Cara.

An unaccustomed feeling of optimism put a spring in Sam's step as he left the exam room. It was almost as if he'd turned a corner in his practice, started down a new—and better—path.

And he knew that he could thank Cara for that, too.

Hands on her hips, Cara surveyed the dining room at the Oak Hill Inn. The tables were draped with white linen and set with silver and crystal. Fresh flowers graced the center of each, and small votive candles awaited the touch of a match, ready to illuminate the room with a warm, romantic glow. Enticing aromas wafted from the kitchen, hinting at the gourmet fare that the opening-night, sell-out crowd would enjoy.

"Pretty amazing, isn't it?"

At Marge's comment, Cara turned. "I can't believe we managed to pull this off in such a short time. But the credit for that goes to you." The innkeeper had handled all the logistics, including rounding up servers and kitchen help, while Cara focused on the food.

"Not at all. It was a team effort. I told you people in this area were hungry for upscale dining. Pardon the pun." The woman gave a hearty laugh, and Cara chuckled in reply. "We're sold out for the next two weekends, too. I'm deferring people after that, until I line up a permanent chef."

"How's the search going?"

"I have a couple of prospects. No one with your credentials, though. It's too bad you can't stay a bit longer."

"I wish I could. But I'm getting pressure from my boss in Philly." He'd called a week ago, pressing her for a return date and hinting that while he understood her need for a leave to recover from the shooting, he couldn't hold her job forever. Cara had promised to return in early August.

She knew she should be grateful he'd given her this much time off. But she couldn't seem to dredge up much enthusiasm about going back to the job she'd once loved. Working here, in an environment where she had total control over menu, presentation and ambience, had been such fun that she didn't relish bowing to the dictates of the often tyrannical executive chef at the restaurant in Philadelphia.

But she couldn't find an excuse to stay. The memories of the shooting had receded, and she was getting out on a frequent basis now. She continued to stay close to Sam's house at night, but she was confident that she'd be okay going home from the inn alone when the restaurant closed for the evening. She was less sure how she'd feel about wandering around at night in the city, but she couldn't hide in Oak Hill forever. She'd just have to deal with any lingering phobias when she returned.

The front door of the inn opened, admitting the first diners, and Marge grinned at Cara. "Here we go!"

For the next two hours, Cara didn't have a second to think about anything but food. With the help of a trained cook they'd been lucky to lure from an eatery in a nearby town, Cara went into high gear in the kitchen. She reviewed every plate before it went out, tweaking the presentation in between directing the servers, who were college students from Rolla.

It was a blur of activity, and by the time dessert was served, she began to feel the effects of the fast pace. She was always tired after her shift in Philadelphia, too. But at least there, the whole dining experience didn't rest on her shoulders. Yet the sense of exhilaration and satisfaction here far surpassed anything she'd ever experienced in previous jobs.

"They're raving about everything, Cara." Marge stuck her head in the kitchen. "And they're asking for you."

With a quick, efficient movement, Cara finished shaving some chocolate onto the last serving of mousse and handed it to the waiting server. After wiping her hands on a towel, she followed Marge into the dining room.

As she entered and scanned the crowd, she was greeted by a spontaneous round of applause, led by Marge. Since she'd looked over the reservation list earlier, she already knew that the locals had turned out in force as a show of support. The sheriff was there with his daughter in tow, as was Reverend Andrews and his wife. A number of the ladies who had worked on the Fourth of July booth had booked the large table in the library. Even portly Gus had come to sample the competition's fare, leaving the diner in someone else's hands for the night.

Sam had come, too, as promised, and his warm smile brought a flush to her cheeks.

When the applause died down and the expectant faces remained fixed on her, Cara realized that she was supposed to say something. Unaccustomed to being in the spotlight, she kept her comments brief. "I'd… um…like to thank everyone for coming. Marge and I are very grateful for your support, and we invite you to return—often. Enjoy your dessert."

An hour later, after the kitchen had been restored to order, the last diner had departed and the staff had headed home, Cara flexed her shoulders as Marge bustled in.

"I'd say our grand opening was a resounding success," the innkeeper declared with a grin.

Smiling, Cara zipped open her purse. "It did go well, didn't it?"

"Now there's an understatement if ever I heard one. I predict that the phone will be ringing off the hook all week with people clamoring to make reservations. Too bad I have to put them off until I line up a new chef." The woman tilted her head and studied Cara. "Is there *anything* I can do to convince you to stay on?"

It was the first time Marge had proposed a permanent arrangement, though she'd hinted at it often enough.

With regret, Cara shook her head. "I have a good job waiting for me back home. And my life is there. This was never intended to be anything more than a brief… getaway."

"Too bad. You fit in well in Oak Hill. And Dr. Martin sure seems glad to have you around." She gave Cara an appraising look. "Remember when I told you that he could use a little lightening up? And that the folks here would like him to chat more, the way old Doc Adams did? Well, since you've been in town, I've been hearing positive things about the changes in him. That he's talking to his patients now, letting them know he cares about more than just the ache or pain he's treating that day. I have to believe you had a lot to do with that. You're good for him, you know."

A shadow of remembered pain darkened Cara's eyes for an instant. "There's a lot of history between us, Marge. This was a pleasant interlude, but it's much more difficult to sustain harmony long term."

"It does take work, that's a fact. My Stan used to say that the best marriages are like a polished theatrical presentation. What the world sees looks easy, but the actors have spent hours and hours rehearsing behind the scenes, getting their timing down so they can roll with the punches when things don't go quite the way they expected once they're onstage. He was right, God rest his soul."

Digging into her purse for her keys, Cara dipped her chin, unsure how to respond. Especially now that she knew a bit of the history of Marge's marriage. She admired the woman's ability to forgive the wrongs and focus on the good things.

"Well, now, enough philosophy for tonight." Marge smiled, picking up the slack in the conversation. "This was a grand evening. We should celebrate."

"I'd love to, but I'm beat." Cara snagged her keys and checked her watch. It was only eleven, but she'd been at the restaurant since one, and the days leading up to the opening had been long and hectic. "Besides, we have to repeat this tomorrow night. It's off to bed for me."

"I suppose I should do the same, considering I have to be up at the crack of dawn to cook breakfast for my guests. By the way, Dr. Martin's waiting for you out front."

"Sam's still here?" Cara gave the innkeeper a startled look.

"Mmm-hmm." Marge gestured toward the foyer. "He said he wanted to follow you home. As if he has to worry about your safety in Oak Hill."

It was clear from her skeptical tone that the woman didn't buy his explanation, seeing it instead as an excuse to be with his estranged wife. And Cara didn't enlighten her about her problem with darkness, either. She'd managed to avoid going out at night alone ever since arriving in Oak Hill. Tonight would have been her first solo venture. She'd felt sure she could handle it, but in truth she wasn't sorry Sam had waited. It had taken all of her energy to get through the opening. It was a relief not to have to tackle the challenge of darkness until tomorrow.

Instead of addressing Marge's comment, she smiled and redirected the conversation. "I'll see you tomorrow afternoon."

"I'll be here." Marge turned toward the door leading to the foyer. "Shall I send Dr. Martin back?"

"Yes, thanks."

Marge disappeared through the door, and less than a minute later Sam stepped through. Once again, his smile warmed her—as did his words.

"That was a fabulous dinner, Cara."

A flush of pleasure washed over her. "Thank you. But you didn't have to wait for me."

"I thought you might like some company on the way home. It's pretty late."

He didn't mention her fear, but she saw the unspoken message in his eyes, along with caring and empathy. She hadn't had a panic attack since the night of the garlic episode, and she'd hate to mar the exhilaration of this evening's success with another such incident.

"I appreciate your consideration. After all the excitement of the past few days, it's nice not to have to deal with any more stress tonight."

"Are you parked in back?"

At her nod, he stepped past her and opened the rear door, waiting until she passed through before following. After she locked up, he fell into step beside her, his hand resting lightly at the small of her back, in a protective gesture that Cara found way too appealing. For a brief second, an almost overwhelming temptation swept over her to lean into the solid strength of his body, as she had often done in the early days of their relationship. But she squelched the impulse. Nevertheless, she missed his touch when they reached her car and he withdrew his hand.

"I'm parked in front. I'll wait for you at the end of the driveway."

In silence, she slid into the driver's seat and locked her door. In the rearview mirror, she watched him stride around the side of the inn and disappear into the darkness.

Once he was out of sight, the blackness around her suddenly became oppressive. Every shadow took on a sinister shape, and she felt the stomach-clenching terror begin to grip her. Her pulse accelerated, and as she tried to insert the key into the ignition she realized that her hand was shaking. A film of moisture broke out on her forehead, and her respiration grew erratic.

So much for thinking she'd conquered her irrational fear of darkness, Cara reflected in dismay as the familiar symptoms of a panic attack began to intensify.

Forcing herself to take deep, slow breaths, she gritted her teeth, determined not to succumb to the waves of groundless fear that were washing over her. Over and over she repeated the same phrases to herself. *There's nothing to be afraid of. Sam is within calling distance. This is a safe town, and no one is going to hurt me.*

Cara wasn't sure how long she sat there, reciting that mantra in silence. But at a sudden gentle tap on her window, her slowing pulse skyrocketed again and she jerked her head toward the glass.

The dim illumination in the inn's small parking lot threw the lines of worry on Sam's face into sharp relief. He motioned for her to unlock her door, and with fumbling fingers she complied. Sam reached for the handle and pulled it open, leaning down.

"Are you okay?"

"Y-yes." A single-word answer was all she could manage.

"I've been waiting for five minutes."

Had she been struggling to gain control for that long? Somehow she'd lost track of time once the panic had begun to suffocate her.

"I'm sorry. I was…I didn't expect…this is my first venture out alone at night. I thought I'd be okay. And I would have been. I was getting it under c-control. It just took me a few minutes."

His gaze shifted to her white-knuckled grip on the wheel. "Let me drive you home."

"No." The refusal came out too strong, and too angry, judging by his startled reaction. But she wasn't angry with Sam; she was upset with herself. Cara took a deep breath and tried again. "I'm sorry. I didn't mean to snap. It's just that I need to get over this. I'm going home in two weeks. I have to be able to function at night by myself."

"Panic attacks aren't that easy to control."

"Tell me about it." Tears of frustration caught her by surprise, stinging her eyes, and she blinked them away. "Can we try this again?"

Instead of responding, he covered her cold hand with his. He could feel the tremors in her fingers, could sense the shudders that rippled through her body. He debated whether to argue with her about driving, but he doubted they'd see any other cars at this hour, especially on a Thursday night. And maybe driving herself the short distance home would give her a needed boost of confidence.

"Yes. I'm parked at the end of the driveway." With an encouraging squeeze of her fingers, he stood. After closing her door he strode away, disappearing into the shadows.

This time, Cara managed to turn the key, put the car in gear and ease down the inn's driveway. True to his word, Sam was waiting. As she drove down the dark road, she had only to glance in the rearview mirror to know he was close behind. His presence calmed her, and she felt much more in control when they pulled into his driveway.

He joined her as she stepped from the car, scrutinizing her face. "Okay?"

"Yes, thanks. Sorry about this."

"There's no need to apologize, Cara. There was a good chance this would happen on your first attempt to go out alone at night. But that doesn't mean it will become a pattern."

"Is that why you waited? Because you thought I might have a panic attack?"

"That was one of the reasons." He wasn't about to go into the other one, that it would buy him a few precious minutes in his wife's company. During the past couple of weeks, as she and Marge had plunged into preparations for the opening, he'd been delighted to watch her old sparkle return, and he was glad she seemed to be putting the shooting behind her. But he'd seen far less of her. And in two short weeks, she planned to leave Oak Hill.

Soon he'd have to share with her what was in his heart, despite the risk. Until he did, however, he'd steal whatever time she could spare, hoping that opportunity would knock and open the door to the conversation he knew they needed to have.

Her pensive expression told him that she was trying to figure out his enigmatic answer. To distract her, he once more placed his hand at the small of her back and urged her toward the house. "It's late, and you've had a long day. Let's go in."

In silence, she followed his lead, speaking only when they entered the kitchen and he flipped the light on.

"Thanks again, Sam."

"My pleasure. Any lingering effects from the little episode in the parking lot?"

"No. I think we headed off the attack at the pass. It never escalated past the first stage."

"Good. Would you like something to help you sleep?"

"No. I'll be fine." Sam's presence in the house, mere steps away, would do more than any sedative to ease her mind and relax her. She had no fears for her physical safety with him close by.

Her emotional safety was another story, however.

In the weeks she'd spent in his house, Cara had become convinced that Sam had truly changed. The arrogance and anger and bitterness that had driven them apart seemed to have been replaced by humility and kindness and compassion. As a result, she was falling in love all over again with her husband. But could she trust that the changes in him were permanent?

"Good night, Cara."

Pausing at the kitchen door, Cara turned—and the unguarded yearning on Sam's face took her breath away. If she was reading him correctly, he'd like nothing better than to close the distance between them and take her in his arms.

As unsettling as that notion was, her own feelings were even more unnerving. She, too, wanted to recapture the closeness they'd once shared, long ago.

Frightened by the powerful surge of longing that shook the foundation of her world, Cara took an abrupt step back. "Good night."

Then she turned and fled down the hall.

And as she closed her door behind her and leaned against it, she knew that the pounding of her heart hadn't been prompted this time by the beginnings of a panic attack. Nor did she expect it to subside soon. Not when the longing in Sam's eyes was emblazoned on her mind.

Perhaps she should have taken him up on his offer of a sedative, after all.

Chapter Twelve

At the sound of the doorbell the following Monday night, Sam stopped scrubbing the pot in his hands and grabbed a dish towel.

"Would you like me to get it?" Cara looked up from some notes she was writing at the kitchen table for the second weekend's dinners at the inn.

Eyeing his soapy hands, he gave her a hopeful look. "Would you mind?"

"Not at all."

Peering through the side window as she approached, Cara was surprised to see Dale Lewis on the porch. Grasping the handle, she swung the front door wide and smiled. "Hello, Sheriff."

"Cara. Sorry to bother you in the evening, but it was easier to stop on my way home."

"No problem. How's Jenna?"

"Doing much better, thanks. Dr. Martin did a great job sewing her up. It's healing so well I doubt there will be any scar."

"I'm glad to hear it. Would you like to come in? We just finished dessert, but I think I could manage to find you a piece of apple cobbler if you're hungry."

He flashed her a quick smile. "That's a tempting offer, but I'm already late picking up Jenna. I wouldn't have stopped, but I need to take care of some official business and I thought it would be better to handle this in person."

"Oh. Well, let me get Sam for you."

"Actually, it's you I came to see."

Turning back to look at him, her expression was quizzical—and cautious.

"May I come in for a moment?"

"Yes. Of course." She stepped aside, giving him room to enter, then shut the door behind him. "Would you like to sit down?"

"I won't be here but a couple of minutes. I wanted to let you know I had a call from the Philadelphia Police Department today."

Cara felt the room suddenly tilt. Since coming to Oak Hill, she'd done a good job of burying the memories of the shooting in the far recesses of her mind. And there'd been nothing here to stir them up. Until now.

"Sheriff. This is a surprise." Sam entered the room, wiping his hands on the dish towel. But his welcoming smile faded when he glanced at Cara. The color had drained from her face, and he could tell even from across the room that she was trembling, suggesting that a panic attack was imminent. He closed the distance between them in a few long strides, putting a protective arm around her shoulders as he led her to the couch in the living room.

"What's going on?" He directed the question over his shoulder to Dale.

"I had a call from the Philadelphia Police Department today. I wanted to alert Cara that they'd be contacting her tomorrow."

Easing Cara down onto the couch, Sam sat beside her, keeping an arm around her shoulders. "About the shooting?"

"Yes." Dale turned the straight chair in the living room at right angles to the couch, near Cara. Sitting, he leaned forward and clasped his hands between his knees. "I know that was a very traumatic experience, Cara, and I'm sorry to have to bring this up. But there was another incident a couple of day ago, very similar to the one in which you were involved. This time they have a suspect in custody. They've asked me to moderate a conference call at my office tomorrow so that they can ask you a few more questions, in the hope that you might remember something that will link this person to the shooting and robbery at your restaurant."

"I don't know anything that can help them." Cara's voice came out tight and choked. "The man was masked. I never saw his face."

"I know. The Philly police filled me in." Dale kept his tone quiet and conversational. "But often, when people have recovered a bit from their trauma, they can be prompted to remember little details that might be helpful in identifying a perpetrator. That's why they'd like to talk with you again."

As Cara listened to Dale, memories of her one

session with the Philadelphia police flashed through her mind in vivid, upsetting detail. At their request, she'd gone to the station to talk with the investigating officers. Liz had accompanied her, though her friend had stayed outside during the official interview…such as it was. The officers hadn't gotten much. As she'd begun describing the events of that night, she'd been gripped by such a severe panic attack that they'd had to send for a doctor. It had taken her days to recover.

Cara swallowed and shook her head. "I can't do it," she whispered.

His blue eyes intent, Dale leaned closer. "They need your input, Cara. It could help bring justice to the man who killed your coworker."

Feeling trapped, she turned to Sam, her panicked expression telegraphing her fear.

He brushed the hair back from her face, his touch tender, his eyes filled with compassion. "You can do this, Cara. You're strong enough to handle it."

Was she? Cara didn't think so. The odds were high that a discussion with the Philly police would induce another severe panic attack. Yet she wanted to do her part to bring justice to Tony's killer. She just wasn't sure she was up to it.

As the silence lengthened, Dale cleared his throat. "I need to be going. The only reason for my visit tonight was to alert you that they'd be calling. That's not normal protocol, but knowing the background, I thought it would be better if you were prepared." He rose, directing his next comment to Sam. "Why don't you show me out?" He nodded toward the door.

Picking up the sheriff's cue, Sam rose. "Sit tight, Cara. I'll be right back."

When Dale stepped outside, Sam followed, closing the door behind him with a soft click.

"I'd feel more comfortable if you came along tomorrow," Dale told him. "According to the Philly police, Cara fell apart during the last questioning session. They had to send for a doctor."

Sam's gut clenched, and he shoved his hands into his pockets. "She's been suffering from panic attacks ever since the shooting. I've witnessed one severe episode, and she's come close to having attacks on a couple of other occasions. Forcing her to dredge up memories of the incident could very well bring on another one."

"That's why I'd like you to be there."

His expression troubled, Sam raked his fingers through his hair. "Are they sure this is necessary? If the man was masked, what can she tell them?"

"You'd be amazed at what we can ferret out of people who think they don't remember anything. But the key is to make them feel comfortable. And secure. I'll do my best to create a safe environment tomorrow, and the investigating officers are aware that the questioning needs to be handled with kid gloves. Your presence would help a lot."

"If Cara wants me to come along, I'll be there."

"Fair enough. She can expect a call first thing in the morning. And now I have a hungry four-year-old to fetch." With a brief smile and a wave he turned and strode down the walk.

When Sam returned to the living room, Cara was still

sitting on the couch, arms crossed in a closed posture, her complexion far too pale. Panic continued to lurk in the depths of her eyes, and when Sam took his seat beside her again she turned to him.

"I'll have another panic attack if I pull up all those memories, Sam."

Her agitated tone convinced him that she was close to having one now. And that there was a good probability she'd have one tomorrow.

"Would it help if I came along?"

Surprise—and relief—registered in her features. "Yes! If you can spare the time."

"I'll make the time." His gaze locked with hers, and he reached out to trace the graceful curve of her cheek with a tentative finger. Her eyes widened, and he heard her soft indrawn breath, but she didn't pull back.

A mere whisper away, he could see the gold flecks in her deep green eyes and the faint sprinkling of freckles across the bridge of her nose. His focus dropped to her lips, slightly parted and oh-so-appealing, and all at once memories of their first kiss came rushing back.

It had been late, after her shift ended at the restaurant. He'd picked her up and driven her home. After spending hours in the kitchen, she'd smelled of exotic spices, he recalled. He'd walked her to her door, planning to say a simple good-night, when she'd turned to look up at him with such warmth and welcome that he'd been left with no choice but to claim her lips.

Her lips still called to him, and the urge to claim them was as strong now as it had ever been. Dare he take the risk?

Sam looked to Cara for an answer to that question, waiting for some signal that she would welcome his kiss. Praying for it. When it came, in a subtle softening of her features, he knew that this was the moment he'd been waiting for. And despite the fear that gripped him like a powerful vise, he couldn't turn back. The time had come to let Cara see what was in his heart.

The first touch of their lips was as sweet as the homecoming of a long-absent loved one. There was a sense of rightness, of completeness in it. Here, in Cara's arms, he had come home.

The kiss felt like a homecoming to Cara, too. And reminded her that she'd been privy to a side of Sam he'd shared with no one else. He'd never been demonstrative in public. But in private, he'd exhibited a depth of emotion that had surprised—and delighted—her, revealing feelings that ran deep and strong. Love had brought out the best in him.

Until a few weeks ago, Cara had been certain that the damage to their marriage could never be repaired. But in suffering her own trauma, she'd learned about the depths of despair that such an ordeal could evoke. She'd begun to understand how desperation could drive a person to take extraordinary—and out-of-character—measures to escape, to find relief. To appreciate how despair and hopelessness could warp a personality. She'd begun to believe that his date with the waitress hadn't been so much betrayal as desperation, driven by anguish and depression. And his contrition seemed real.

The ball was now in her court. Was she willing to

forgive? To take the risk of loving, when there were no guarantees?

As the kiss moved from tender to powerful, Cara stopped thinking. In the arms of the only man she'd ever loved, she let her heart take the lead and gave herself freely to his kiss. There would be time enough later for her mind to deal with uncertainty. For this moment, she let her heart speak.

To her surprise, it was Sam who finally broke contact, easing back to rest his forehead against hers.

"I didn't plan this for tonight, Cara. But I knew it was coming." His voice was hoarse as he cradled her head in his hands, their foreheads touching, his fingers tangled in her hair.

"So did I," she whispered, clinging to him like a sailor holding fast to the mast in a stormy sea.

They stayed like that for another minute, and then Sam backed up enough to search her face. "This isn't the best timing, though. Not with tomorrow's ordeal looming."

He was right. She was scared and vulnerable and in need of comfort, and he'd recognized that. Her precarious emotional state wasn't the only reason she'd sought shelter in his arms, however. But she wasn't up to discussing the other reasons tonight.

Extricating herself from his embrace, she stood. "I think I'll read for a while in my room before I go to bed."

"Cara, I know you have the police interview on your mind tonight, but we do need to talk."

She played with the cording on the edge of the couch. "I know. We will. I just…I need some time."

"You're leaving in two weeks."

"I know that, too."

"I don't want you to go, Cara."

His candid admission surprised her, and the trace of desperation in his voice tugged at her heart. But she couldn't deal with their future tonight. She had to get through tomorrow first. And she needed to do a whole lot more praying. She'd been asking the Lord for guidance almost from the day she'd arrived in Oak Hill, and Marge's story had been inspiring, but clear direction for her own situation continued to elude her.

Yet she knew her thinking was undergoing a change. In view of Sam's sincere remorse, she now knew that forgiveness was within her grasp. And that she still loved the man she'd married. Perhaps more than ever, considering the appealing changes in him. But love didn't guarantee a happy ending, as their relationship up until now proved. And she couldn't survive a second breakup. It was that fear that made her wary.

"I'm sorry, Sam. I need a few more days." It was the best she could do tonight, but his disheartened expression told her he had hoped for more.

Nevertheless, he pulled himself together and managed to dredge up the semblance of a smile. "Does this whole scene strike you as a bit ironic? The last few years we were together, you were always the one who wanted to have deep discussions, and I was the one who pushed you off. All of a sudden I'm getting a sense of how frustrating that must have been for you."

"It was very hard, Sam. A lot of things were." She looked at him steadily, no answering smile touching her lips. "You know what was hardest to deal with at the end? Your anger. I didn't know you were capable of such rage. Or such loss of control. I'll never forget the night you broke the goblet. I was almost…afraid of you." Cara's voice shook on the last three words.

Shocked, Sam stared at the woman he loved. He, too, could recall that night in vivid detail. His clumsy hand had lost its grip on a fragile goblet he'd retrieved from a cabinet in the kitchen, and though he'd struggled to grab it, it had hit the edge of the counter and cracked. He'd exploded, uttering a word that had made Cara cringe as he hurled it against the wall, smashing it into a thousand pieces. He'd sensed her shocked withdrawal, felt her self-protective mechanism slip into place. But he hadn't cared at the time. Nor had he realized that his violent response would have such a lasting impact.

All at once, one of Liz's comments from their phone conversation weeks before echoed in his mind. She'd warned him that Cara couldn't handle his anger. The significance hadn't registered then, but it did now. Cara must have shared her fears with Liz.

His wife had been afraid of him.

He felt as if someone had kicked him in the gut.

"I had no idea you felt that way." The words came out hoarse and ragged, and he raked shaky fingers through his hair. "I was in a lot of emotional pain, and I was angry at everyone and everything, but…Cara, I would never, ever have done anything to hurt you physically."

Her silence told Sam that she wasn't sure she could believe him. And that was like a second kick. "I'm sorry, Cara. For all my mistakes. I promise you it would be different this time."

"Look, give me a few days, okay? We'll talk then."

Realizing that the subject was closed for now, he gave a resigned nod. "If you have trouble sleeping tonight, let me know."

"Thanks."

Left alone, Sam's shoulders drooped as he lowered his head into his hands. He was asking a lot of Cara. Perhaps too much. She'd put up with him when he was inattentive, endured his arrogance, suffered through his bitterness. Even lived in fear at the end, as he'd just been appalled to learn.

Despite all his faults, she'd kept loving him, believing that somewhere, deep inside him, the man she'd fallen in love with still lived. And he'd repaid her loyalty and love by coming dangerously close to violating the vows of fidelity they'd taken on the day they were wed. In light of that ultimate betrayal, it was no wonder she had left him.

As Sam examined the stark, ugly reality of his behavior, his spirits plummeted. How could he expect Cara to forgive him for all he'd done to destroy their relationship? He couldn't even forgive himself.

Yet how could he go on if she didn't?

Chapter Thirteen

The Oak Hill Police Department was nothing like the busy, noisy precinct headquarters she'd visited with Liz in Philadelphia, Cara noted in relief as Dale ushered her into his homey office. Multiple pictures of Jenna were displayed on the oak bookshelves that took up most of one wall. A large picture window looked out over the tree-shaded yard next door, where colorful zinnias seemed oblivious to the late-July heat and humidity, already oppressive at ten in the morning. The seat Dale led her to was upholstered and comfortable, unlike the wooden, straight-backed chair in Philly. And there was another important difference, too.

This time, Sam was by her side.

"Can I get you some water, Cara?"

Turning, she managed to give Dale a tremulous smile as she sat. "Yes, thanks." She twisted her hands in her lap and tried to focus on one of the carefree, smiling photos of Jenna, determined to get through this without falling apart.

As she angled her head, Sam assessed her, his expression concerned. Despite his request, she'd refused to eat any breakfast. And the dark smudges under her eyes, their sooty color emphasized by her pallor, indicated that she'd slept very little. The rapid rise and fall of her chest, her clenched hands, and the tautness of her features told him she was hanging on to her composure by a thread.

"I talked to Philly again first thing this morning to go over the procedure." Dale reentered the room and handed her a bottle of cold water. As he spoke, he positioned the speakerphone in the middle of his desk and retrieved another chair from the hall outside his office, which he placed near Cara's. "Two detectives will be on the call. Chad Miller and Mark Fernandez. I believe Chad was one of the officers who spoke with you after the shooting."

"Yes." Cara had only a vague recollection of the detective. All her memories of that traumatic interview were hazy.

"They'll want you to walk through the events that took place that night, guided by their questions. It might be good to close your eyes as you do that, to help you focus. Total concentration can often bring back details that could be important."

At the sudden ring of the phone, Cara's hand jerked and she dropped the unopened bottle of water. Dale bent to retrieve it, setting it by her chair, as Sam reached for her hand. When she looked his way, he entwined his fingers with hers and gave them a gentle squeeze.

For the first couple of minutes, Dale spoke into the

receiver. Then he punched a button to activate the speakerphone and took his seat. "We're set on this end."

"Ms. Martin? Detective Miller. We met several weeks ago."

"I remember."

"Thank you for speaking with us today. For the record, we'll be recording this conversation."

"Detective Fernandez here, Ms. Martin. As you know, we're investigating what appear to be related incidents. We're hoping our conversation with you might turn up some new information that will link the suspect from the most recent crime to the one you were involved in. This robbery occurred in the same vicinity as the restaurant where you work, and the victim was able to give us some helpful information that allowed us to make an arrest. The similarities between the crimes lead us to believe that they're linked."

"We know this is difficult for you, so we'll try to do it as quickly as we can," Detective Miller added. "I understand that in addition to the sheriff, Dr. Martin is also in the room. Dr. Martin, can you verify that for the record?"

"Yes. This is Sam Martin."

"All right. Let's get started," the detective continued. "We'd like you to tell us what happened, beginning with your exit from the restaurant that night, Ms. Martin. Give us every detail you remember—nothing is too small to ignore. We may interrupt with a few questions as you go along. We're in no hurry, so take your time. Please begin whenever you're ready."

Fighting down the panic bubbling up inside her, Cara looked at the sheriff, who gave her an encouraging nod.

On her other side, Sam squeezed her hand and edged his chair a bit closer. Recalling the sheriff's advice, Cara took a deep breath and closed her eyes. *Please, Lord, help me get through this without breaking down. And help me remember something that will assist these men in bringing Tony's killer to justice.*

Slowly, in a halting, unsteady voice, Cara began to recount the events of the attack, struggling all the while to rein in her panic, to slow her pulse, to control the nausea that threatened to gag her. When she came to the part where the assailant grabbed her, however, the words caught in her throat and her eyes flew open. She tried to draw in some air, but her lungs seemed frozen. She gasped, and her grip tightened on Sam's hand.

"Hold on a second, guys." Dale directed his comment toward the phone while he picked up her water, twisting off the cap as he shot Sam a worried look.

"Cara, it's okay." Sam leaned close, smoothing the hair back from her damp forehead. He'd brought some medication with him, but he'd prefer not to use it if he could talk her through this and avert a full-fledged attack. "Take a slow, deep breath. Come on, do it with me, sweetheart. Breathe in…good…hold it…okay, now let it out slow and easy. Good. Let's do that again."

Within a couple of minutes, Cara's breathing steadied, and some of the tension in her features eased. When Sam reached for the water bottle, Dale handed it over. He put it up to Cara's lips, and her hand closed over his. "Take a drink, sweetheart. I'll help you." Together they tilted the bottle, and Cara took a long swallow. When they lowered the bottle, Sam gave her an assessing look. "Do you think you can continue?"

"I— I'll try."

Although her grip on his hand had loosened, her fingers were still ice cold. He moved his chair even closer and slipped his free arm around her shoulders before nodding to Dale.

"Okay, guys, we're ready to continue," the sheriff said.

Sam's solid body pressed close beside her, and the protective circle of his arm, gave Cara the courage to go on. As she described the way the man had grabbed her and pressed the barrel of the gun to her head, Detective Miller interrupted.

"Ms. Martin, could you recount the conversation for us word for word at this point, as best you can remember?"

Swallowing, Cara forced herself to concentrate, letting the verbal exchange replay in her mind instead of thinking about the terror of that cold metal against her temple. "The man said to Tony, 'Don't try to be no macho hero, man. Just give me the money or this little lady ain't gonna see tomorrow. And neither will you.' When Tony took out his wallet, the guy said, 'That's better. Put it on the ground and kick it my direction.' After Tony did that, the guy laughed and said, 'Okey-doke. Now you're being smart.'"

"Could you repeat that last line, Ms. Martin?" Detective Fernandez said.

"He said, 'Okeydoke. Now you're being smart.'"

"Thank you. Please continue."

"He shoved me to the ground and reached for the wallet. Tony lunged for him. They scuffled, and he...he fired the gun. Tony fell. The man didn't say anything else. He just moved toward me and…pointed the gun in my direction. He looked at me for several seconds. I thought he…was going to shoot me, too. But he r-ran off instead." By the end of Cara's recitation, her words were choppy, and she was starting to have trouble breathing again.

"We're going to take another little break here, guys," Dale said toward the speaker.

"No problem. We'll wait."

Hearing Cara recount the trauma in all its horror, watching fear distort her features as she spoke of facing death, realizing how close he had come to losing her, had been like a knife twisting in Sam's stomach. Her whole body was trembling and, despite Sam's aversion to public displays of affection, he rose and pulled her up beside him, wrapping his arms around her in a comforting embrace, pressing her head against his chest.

"It's okay. Take some long, slow breaths like you did before and you'll be fine, sweetheart. We're almost finished here." He sent a questioning glance over her shoulder to Dale, who confirmed the statement with a nod.

Not until her trembling subsided and her respiration had regulated did Sam loosen his embrace. Backing up, he searched her pale face. "Are you up to continuing?"

"Yes."

He released her, but this time *she* reached for *his* hand, clutching it tightly as she retook her seat.

"Okay, guys. Dale here. What else do you need? I'm not sure we can keep this up much longer."

"We only have a couple more questions," Detective

Miller assured them. "You've been very helpful, Ms. Martin. Now I'd like you to focus on the gun. Picture it in the assailant's hand. Take a minute to review that in your mind. See if there's anything distinctive you can tell us."

"I don't know anything about guns, Detective."

"That's okay. Humor us on this. Think of how it looked in his hand, and any motions he might have made with it."

Puzzled, Cara once more closed her eyes. She thought of the man brandishing the gun at them when he popped out from behind a car in the parking lot. Remembered the glint off the metal barrel, a reflection from the security light overhead. Pictured it pointed at Tony and her. Felt the metal pressed to her forehead after he'd grabbed her, his arm so tight against her throat as he pulled her against him that she could hardly breathe. Visualized it aimed at her as she cowered on the ground, less than two feet away from the deadly barrel.

But then, to her surprise, she saw something else. In the scuffle with Tony, the man's shirt must have ripped, because she could see his forearm now. As well as a tattoo, illuminated by the overhead light.

Her eyes flew open, and she gasped. Instantly, Sam leaned close, searching her face. "Cara? Are you okay?"

"Yes. I just remembered that the man had a tattoo."

"Can you describe it?" The intensity in Detective Fernandez's voice wasn't lost on anyone in the room.

Squeezing her eyes shut again, Cara once more pictured the scene. "The overhead security light was shining on it. It was on his right arm, above his wrist. Two colors. Blue and orange. It looked like some kind of bird." She tried to come up with more detail, but it eluded her. "I'm sorry. That's all I can remember."

"That's more than enough," Detective Miller told her. "You've been a great help today. Both the tattoo and the unusual slang expression are valuable links between the two assaults. That's all we need for now. Sheriff Lewis, Dr. Martin, thank you both for assisting. And special thanks to you, Ms. Martin. I know this was difficult for you."

After wrapping up the call, Dale turned to Cara. "You did a remarkable job."

"Your coaching helped. When I closed my eyes, I did remember some things that I didn't realize I'd noticed. How did you know that would work?"

"I spent a lot of years on the police force in L.A. and I picked up a few tricks along the way." He turned to Sam. "Your presence today was invaluable. Thank you for coming."

"I couldn't have been anywhere else." His gaze was on Cara when he spoke. "Are you ready to go?"

"Yes."

They left the station in silence, and when Sam slid into the driver's seat after closing Cara's door, she turned to him.

"Thank you for coming, Sam. I'm sorry I disrupted your morning."

"As I told the sheriff, I couldn't have been anywhere else."

She checked her watch, not up to exploring the implications of that comment. She'd promised Sam they'd talk, but this wasn't the time. A sudden weariness was sweeping over her, an aftermath of her restless night and the stress of the interview. "At least you'll be able to salvage most of your appointments for today."

"I canceled everything."

Surprised, she turned to him. "Why?"

"I wanted to be available in case you needed m… anything. Given the circumstances, there was a strong possibility you could have had a panic attack. But you did great, Cara. You're beating this thing. Today should give you a lot of confidence that you're on the road to recovery."

"I'm not sure I could have gotten through it if you hadn't been there."

Her soft comment warmed him. "I'm glad I could be there to support you." As he turned into his drive-way, he caught Cara trying to stifle a yawn. "Someone needs a nap."

"I am tired. But it doesn't seem right that I should go to bed when you've taken the whole day off to be with me."

He set the brake and turned to her. "Trust me, Cara. I'm ecstatic that you'll be sleeping peacefully instead of fighting the aftereffects of a panic attack." He touched her cheek, letting his fingers linger for several seconds before he retracted his hand and lightened his tone. "Besides, you need the rest. You have another big weekend coming up. Marge tells me the dining room is sold out again."

"Yes. This weekend and next. Are you coming again?"

"Every night."

Stunned, she stared at him. "You're kidding."

"Where else could I get a better meal? You've spoiled

me these past few weeks. I'm not sure I can go back to those frozen dinners. Or Gus's."

The compliment pleased her. But as she opened her mouth to respond, another yawn caught her unaware.

"It's off to bed for you. We can't have Oak Hill's premier chef too tired too cook."

Later, safely snuggled in her bed, Cara thought about one of Sam's earlier remarks. When she'd expressed surprise that he'd changed his schedule to be with her, he'd almost responded by saying that he'd wanted to be available in case she needed him.

And more and more, Cara was becoming convinced that she did need Sam. Not just when she had panic attacks, not just to help her get through difficult situations like today, but for always. To hold her hand in the simple moments of life as well as the stressful ones, to sit with her on the porch swing after a busy day, or share a quiet dinner or an impromptu morning picnic, as they had when she'd first arrived in Oak Hill.

As sleep began to cloud her mind, the sermon Reverend Andrews had given that first Sunday she and Sam had attended services together replayed in her mind. He had pointed out that in a world filled with broken promises and betrayal, it can be difficult to follow the Lord's commandment to love one another as He loved us. And he'd said that love is about sharing and sacrifice, about unselfishness and forgiveness. Not once, but over and over again. He'd also said that in a good marriage, partners must persevere. With trust, and with faith, and with hope.

In the seconds before she fell into a deep sleep, Cara

knew that she was being called to abide by the Lord's directive, to free her heart from troubles and fears. And to follow His example to remain steadfast in love despite human imperfections and failings.

It was time, Cara knew, to listen with an open heart and mind to what her husband had to say. It was time to take a leap of faith and put her trust in the Lord—and in Sam.

As Sam dug into his lemon tart garnished with a generous dollop of whipped cream, the tension of the past few days caught up with him. Since their kiss, he'd been anxious to talk with Cara. In nine days she was scheduled to get on a plane and return to Philadelphia. But they'd had no chance to exchange more than a few words.

After losing a day at the office, he'd been playing catch-up with appointments. A rare spate of emergencies had kept him at the hospital in Rolla for long stretches, and he'd put in extra hours at the volunteer clinic on his day off when more patients than usual showed up.

Cara's schedule had been hectic, too. After recovering from the emotional trauma of the interview on Tuesday with the Philly police, she'd thrown herself into preparations for her second weekend at the inn. And based on the two meals he'd had so far, her personal problems hadn't had any negative impact on her usual stellar performance in the kitchen.

"Miss…" The older man at the next table flagged down his waitress. "Would you ask the chef to come out when she has a minute?"

"Of course, sir."

Watching the exchange, Sam wondered if the couple

had a complaint. He hoped not, after all Cara's hard work. But they didn't look unhappy, he decided. They were smiling at each other, and there was an almost girlish glow on the woman's face.

Out of the corner of his eye, Sam saw Cara come through the kitchen door. She flashed him a quick smile as she passed, but she didn't pause on her way to the table next to his.

"Ah, here she is, Delores."

A delighted smile lit Cara's face as she stopped beside them. "Mr. and Mrs. Wilson! What a wonderful surprise!"

The man and woman held out their hands in turn, and Cara took each in a warm clasp.

"My dear, we're the ones who are surprised," the man told her. "We were passing through town and saw the ad for this restaurant in your local paper. After the wonderful meals we enjoyed at the restaurant in Philadelphia where you worked, Delores and I agreed that we had to stop and have dinner here. In fact, we're staying at the inn. That's how we finagled a reservation despite your sell-out crowd. We're driving to Colorado to visit our daughter and her family for our fiftieth anniversary celebration."

"How wonderful for you. Fifty years—that's quite an accomplishment."

The woman chuckled. "Indeed it is. There were days when we weren't sure we'd make it to twenty-five, let alone fifty, isn't that right, Bill?" Affection softened her features.

"That's a fact. But you helped, you know," he told Cara.

"How did I do that?"

"Well, Delores and I always agreed that it was important to spend time together, and to mark notable occasions in distinctive ways." The man reached across the table and took his wife's hand. "Going out for a nice meal is a great way to do that. And your food is the best we've ever eaten. That's why we came so often to sample your fare."

"Remember that wonderful veal cutlet in lemon butter sauce that we had on our forty-eighth anniversary, Bill?" Delores spoke up. "And we thought it was such a sweet gesture when you came out with a complimentary dessert for us at the end. You made our special day *extra* special Cara. We never forgot that night."

After a few more exchanges about their cross-country trip, Cara slipped back to the kitchen. But long after the conversation ended, it replayed in Sam's mind as he looked around the restaurant, studying the patrons with a fresh perspective.

At one table, a young couple seemed oblivious to the world as they sampled each other's desserts, their hands joined, their heads bent close. At another table, an older couple was breaking bread with a younger couple, and Sam watched as they raised their glasses in a toast. At the big table in the back room a joyous birthday party was in progress, and he glimpsed the guest of honor blowing out the candles on a cake amid much laughter and soft applause.

Although he'd always admired Cara's ability to work magic with food, Sam had never recognized the impact her career had on people's lives. As a surgeon, he'd believed that his lifesaving skills made a far more important contribution to society than his wife's culinary abilities. But if he had saved lives, Cara helped make them worth living.

The insight both startled and depressed him. It seemed that his lack of appreciation for his wife's profession was yet one more way he'd failed the woman he loved.

As Sam returned from rounds in Rolla the next afternoon, he ran into Cara in the driveway, headed to the inn. Their paths had barely crossed since Tuesday, except when he was eating at the restaurant.

"I guess I'll see you later for dinner?" She opened the back door of her car and tossed her tote onto the seat.

"Not tonight, unfortunately."

Surprised, she looked at him as he stopped beside her car. "I thought you said you were coming every night?"

"I'd planned to. But I overheard a young couple talking with Marge last night. They stopped in to try and get a reservation for dinner tonight. Turns out they're on their honeymoon. The restaurant was booked solid, so I offered to give up my table. I figured I could survive without your food for one night."

As she looked at him, an idea took shape in Cara's mind. "If you don't mind sitting in Marge's breakfast nook off the kitchen, you're welcome to eat at the inn. Of course, the ambience won't be quite the same. I can't guarantee a relaxed meal, but at least it won't be fried."

Delighted by the offer, Sam wasted no time accepting. He couldn't care less about the ambience; he'd much rather be in Cara's presence than sitting at a table alone in the dining room, anyway. "That would be great, if you're sure I won't be in the way."

"No. It won't be a problem. But don't expect a lot of attention. Things can get pretty hectic in the kitchen. I may forget you're there."

Even as she said the words, Cara wasn't sure they were true. And six hours later, with Sam ensconced in Marge's breakfast nook, watching the proceedings in the kitchen, she discovered how inaccurate they were. She was acutely conscious of his presence, and at first it took all of her will-power to shift her focus from the man across the room to the Chicken Marseille she was preparing.

But as the evening went on and Cara became en-grossed in preparing the food, orchestrating the servers, monitoring her assistant cook and tweaking the presen-tations, she did forget he was nearby. The hectic tempo and need for absolute concentration didn't allow for the luxury of daydreaming.

As Sam enjoyed his meal, out of the line of action but with a clear view of the activity, he gained yet another insight into Cara's work. She'd often told him, when he expressed surprise that she could maintain her weight despite preparing gourmet food everyday, that kitchens were a busy place and she burned a lot of calories.

He'd always met that response with skepticism. Now he revised his opinion. He was used to seeing her putter around the kitchen at home. The grueling pace of a com-mercial kitchen was a whole different ball game. By the end of the evening, he was tired just from watching her, and he had a whole new respect for her organizational and management abilities. No wonder she'd always looked a bit frustrated when he'd condescendingly scoffed at her comments about the taxing nature of her work.

It seemed his list of infractions kept growing, he thought, his demeanor glum as he stared into the dark depths of his coffee. In her place, he wondered if he'd have stuck with the relationship as long as she had.

"How was the dinner?"

At the sound of Cara's voice, he looked up. Although fatigue had etched fine lines at the corners of her eyes, her face was animated and energized, reminding him of how he'd always looked after surgery. Tired, but exhilarated.

"Great, as usual."

"Good." She gave him a pleased look. "We're in the cleanup phase. You don't need to wait if you don't want to. I've been managing the trip home alone without a problem. And a restaurant kitchen isn't the most relaxing place to sit and enjoy a cup of coffee."

"No, but it's been enlightening." His enigmatic comment raised her eyebrows, but before she could reply, he spoke again. "I'll wait, unless you'd rather I not."

"I'd like that. But I'll be tied up here for at least another forty-five minutes."

"That's not a problem."

By the time she sent the waitresses and the assistant cook home, said good-night to Marge and joined him in the breakfast nook, Sam was finishing his third cup of coffee.

"Would you mind if I have a cup? It would be nice to sit and breathe for a minute."

"Not at all. But won't coffee keep you awake?"

"After this marathon? You've got to be kidding. I'll be asleep the second my head hits the pillow." Retrieving the pot, she filled a mug to the brim. "Would you like some more?"

"Sure." He'd pay for his caffeine binge later, but drinking coffee gave him something to do with his hands.

With a sigh, she sank into the chair beside him. "I always heard that running a restaurant is like being in a Broadway show every night. Now I know why."

As she sipped her coffee, silence descended on the kitchen. Only the tick of a clock on the far wall broke the stillness. It was the first time since Tuesday that they'd had a few quiet minutes to sit together, and Sam wondered if Cara had switched gears and was thinking about them, and their future, as he was. He wasn't going to push the discussion she'd promised to have, but after his recent insights about her profession, he did have a few other things he needed to say.

Clearing his throat, he set his cup down and folded his hands around it. "I made a couple of interesting discoveries these past two nights."

"Oh?" She gave him a curious look over the rim of her mug as she raised it to her lips.

"Mmm-hmm. I overheard that little talk you had with the Wilsons last night."

"They're a sweet couple." A smile toyed at her lips. "They were regulars at the restaurant in Philly. I can't believe they found me in this tiny town, and altered their plans so they could eat at the inn."

"After eavesdropping on your conversation with them, and taking a good, hard look at the other patrons, I can."

She remained silent, her expression curious as she sipped her coffee.

"You know, I used to think surgery was such a hotshot profession. So important to society." Sam gripped his cup with both hands. "But I now realize that what you do is just as important. The memories people take away from the special times you help create will sustain and comfort them their whole life. Surgery could never do that."

For years, Cara had prayed that Sam would recognize the value of her profession and appreciate it. But never in her wildest dreams had she allowed herself to hope that he would understand the reason she found such joy and satisfaction in her work. Yet he'd nailed it dead on.

Before she could collect her wits enough to think of a response, he continued. "And tonight I learned something else. Being a chef is difficult, physically demanding work. You used to tell me that, but I never understood what you meant. Tonight, while I watched you juggle multiple balls without drooping a single one, I realized the incredible stamina and coordination and skill it takes to work in this profession. I'm amazed—and impressed. I'm just sorry that it took me such a long time to recognize that spending all those hours on your feet, working magic with your hands, attending to dozens of details, was as taxing as any surgery I've ever done."

As she stared at Sam, it was hard for Cara to imagine what those two speeches had cost him. Even in their best days, he'd never spoken with such humility or freely admitted being wrong. Nor had he often opened his heart this wide. He'd told her when she arrived in Oak Hill that he was working on his communication skills.

If tonight was any example, he had progressed far more than she'd ever dreamed possible.

It also reminded her that she'd promised him they would discuss their future. Since Tuesday, they'd both been too busy. And despite the fatigue she knew would soon set in after her hectic evening, the mood seemed suddenly right.

Setting her mug on the table with exaggerated care, she took a deep breath and looked at Sam. "I think this might be a good time to talk."

Chapter Fourteen

Although Sam had been waiting for this moment, now that it was upon him the metallic taste of fear turned the flavor of the rich coffee he'd just sipped rancid. Settling his cup on the saucer, he realized that his hands were trembling, and he took a steadying breath. He hadn't expected to have this discussion tonight. But he wasn't about to let the late hour deter him from his mission of convincing her to stay.

"Are you sure you aren't too tired?"

"No. I'm wide-awake from the adrenaline rush of the evening. Unless you'd rather wait."

"No." His response was immediate, but he qualified it, giving her another glimpse into his heart. "To be honest, though…I'm scared."

Once more, Cara was taken aback. Sam had never, ever, admitted to being frightened by anything, just as he had never admitted that he needed help. Even after the attack, when he'd been in both physical and mental pain, he'd kept his feelings inside, struggling to cope on his own. That he was willing to set the stage for this discussion by laying his fears on the table endeared him to her more.

"Me, too," she acknowledged in a soft voice, meeting honesty with honesty.

Needing something solid to hold on to, he once again wrapped his fingers around his cup. "I have a lot to say. But it's hard to know where to start." He tried to smile, but all he could manage was a slight twitch of his lips. "I've had a lot of time to think about a lot of things these past few months, Cara. Especially us. And when I look back, I can't help but wonder why you ever fell in love with me. I was no great bargain. Even before all of our problems began, I wasn't a very good husband. Communication was hard for me, and you deserved someone who was able to open up and share at the deepest levels."

"You tried, Sam. You let me in more, back then. And we had some good times."

"I know. For me, those early days with you were the most wonderful of my life. I couldn't believe someone so caring and compassionate, so fun loving and intelligent and beautiful, had agreed to spend her life with me. I wasn't much into religion in those days, but I used to go to bed at night thanking God for the incredible gift He'd sent me in you."

Awed, she stared at him. "I never knew that."

A rueful expression settled over his face. "That was one of my mistakes. I should have told you. But it was only one of many." He looked down at his coffee and shook his head. "There's so much to apologize for I hardly know where to begin."

His words came out in a hoarse whisper, and he was startled when Cara laid her fingers on his scarred hand, her comforting touch as gentle and warm as a soft summer breeze.

Moved by the gesture of support, Sam looked at her. He could sense that she was receptive. Whether she could forgive him, whether she would agree to give their marriage a second chance, was another matter. But at least she was willing to listen. That was a start.

He swallowed past the lump in his throat, praying that the Lord would help him find the words that would touch her.

"Since I came to Oak Hill, I've taken a long, hard look at my life," he began. "And the picture that emerged wasn't pretty. When we met, I was struggling to get established. The workload hadn't yet grown to unmanageable proportions—nor had my ego. Our relationship was new, and I recognized how much it meant to have someone to love. Those were our good years.

"And then came success. My work took precedence over everything. As my stature grew, so did my arrogance and conceit. I started to feel invincible, better and more important than everyone else. That's why religion wasn't as important to me as it was to you. I didn't think I needed anyone…including God. But over the past several months, I realized that I'm not as self-reliant as I thought. I do need God…and I need you. And I also realized that while I was good at what I did, I wasn't perfect. If I had been, Claire West wouldn't have died."

"You were cleared of wrongdoing in that case, Sam."

"I know. But deep inside, I've always wondered if one of my mistakes led to her death. I should never have gone into the operating room that day. And I shouldn't have stayed as long as I did." Cara might be willing to cut him some slack, as had the medical review board, but Sam wasn't as generous. He would live with the burden of guilt over the deaths of Claire and her husband for the rest of his life. "In any case, I can't change that. And Bill West made sure I never have the chance to mess up an operation again."

In the past, when Sam had spoken of the incident that had robbed him of his career, there had always been an acrid bitterness in his voice. Now, his tone was resigned, threaded with a distant echo of sadness.

"After the attack, my world caved in. Whatever closeness we'd once shared had already been strained by my distant manner and preoccupation and selfishness. Since I had nowhere to go with my anger, you bore the brunt of it. I repaid your compassion with rejection. I know I pushed you away, yet when you'd taken as much as you could and backed off, I felt…forsaken. There's no other word to express it. I can't begin to describe the darkness that swirled around me. I started drinking at that bar… and you know the rest."

Her fingers still rested on his, and he covered them with his other hand, afraid she'd pull back. He needed the physical connection to give him the courage to continue. Looking up, his gaze locked on hers.

"The night our paths crossed at the movie was the first—and only—occasion that I saw that woman outside of the bar, Cara. I was at the lowest point I'd ever been. I wish I could tell you that I would have come to my senses on my own and walked away from her, but I can't guarantee that would have happened. It was like I didn't know who I was anymore. I'd failed as a surgeon. I'd failed as a husband. The future looked bleak. To be honest, I'd begun to think about ending it all.

"But for some reason, every time I was tempted to take that step, I would hear that phrase you loved from the Bible. 'Come to Me, all you who labor and are over-burdened, and I will give you rest.' It was odd, because I'd never been a religious sort of guy. Yet that passage kept popping into my mind.

"So I was trying to hang on, wanting to believe that things would get better. But that evening, I felt like the darkness was closing in on me, that I couldn't make it through another desolate, endless night alone. In fact, I was *afraid* to be alone. And that's how I ended up at the movie."

Swallowing again, he tried to smooth out the rough-ness in his voice. "When I saw your devastated face, it was the wake-up call I needed. In that instant, I realized that the answer to my problems didn't lie in a bottle. Or with some waitress whose last name I didn't even know. It was you I needed. You're the only woman I've ever loved. The only woman I ever *want* to love. But I also knew that I'd burned a lot of bridges, and that it would take a miracle to undo the damage I'd caused. Yet from that moment on, I was determined to put my life in order, to straighten out my priorities and to win back your love."

He leaned closer, his eyes intent and earnest. "I've

done the first two, Cara. I've built a new life, and I understand now what's important. I'll never lose sight of that again. As for winning back your love...I had no idea how to go about that, beyond the letters and messages and flowers that you ignored.

"And then Liz's call came out of the blue. I'm more sorry than I can say that our reunion came at your expense. I wish I could erase the night of the shooting from your memory. But I'm grateful that it brought us together, because it gave me a chance to demonstrate to you how much I've changed. And I'm still changing, Cara. For the better, I hope."

A muscle clenched his jaw, and the pressure of his hand tightened on hers. "I'm not sure, were the situation reversed, that I could do what I'm asking of you. But I'm hoping that you'll give me another chance. If you do, I promise you that our worse days are behind us, and that from this day forward I'll do everything I can to make every tomorrow we share better than the one before. I love you, Cara. And I always will."

As Sam finished, Cara had to blink to keep her tears at bay. She dropped her chin, focusing on the grain pattern in Marge's oak table, the irregular lines representing the tree's growth through the years. Sam's honesty and candor, his willingness to put his heart on the line, touched her in a profound way. His contrition seemed real and sincere.

Nor did she doubt the truth of anything he'd said. His actions over the past few weeks, from his invitation to visit, to the suite he'd prepared for her, to the porch swing, to his presence at the police interview, spoke of his sorrow and his desire to atone for his mistakes. And tonight, he'd found the courage to put into words the feelings he held deep inside.

The choice was hers. Return, alone, to her old life in Philly, or leave the past behind and take a second chance with the man who'd stolen her heart.

For weeks, Cara had known that this exchange was coming. And she'd hoped that when it did, her decision would be clear. But all at once, fear gripped her, the bad memories a powerful deterrent to taking the kind of risk Sam had asked of her.

"If you need to think about this, I understand." Sam's tone was careful and measured, yet when she looked at him she saw the turmoil, the uncertainty, the fear in his eyes. "But I wanted you to know how I felt."

Giving a jerky nod, Cara moistened her dry lips. "If you'd asked me this three or four months ago, I would have turned my back and walked away. But the shooting and the panic attacks gave me some sense of the trauma you suffered.

"Since I've been here, I've also seen evidence of the changes you talk about. You seem to lead a much more balanced life now, with a better sense of priorities. You remind me a lot of the man I fell in love with years ago. Only better."

A brief flicker of hope flared to life in Sam's eyes as she spoke, but he remained silent.

"I believed in the vows we took when we got married, Sam. I still do. But when I walked away, I didn't know you anymore. And I was afraid. I'd seen you short-tempered and annoyed through the years, but not out of control or violent. That night you threw the goblet at the wall still scares me."

Never had Sam regretted that fleeting loss of control more than he did at this moment. It had been the sole occasion when he'd expressed his frustration and rage in a physical way. But he hadn't realized the extent of her fear until her revelation earlier in the week.

"Those days are long past, Cara. It was an aberration, and it hasn't happened again. I'm sorry that I frightened you. I would never, ever have done anything to hurt you."

As doubt and indecision pinched her features, disappointment welled up in Sam. He'd hoped she'd throw herself into his arms and tell him that all was forgiven, that she loved him, too, and wanted to start over. But that kind of thing only happened in romance novels, he supposed. In real life, longstanding hurts and betrayal weren't mitigated by a simple apology and profession of love. She needed to process all he'd said, work through her feelings. And he couldn't blame her. He was asking her to radically alter her life, to trust a man who had betrayed her. It was a huge step, and he needed to give her space.

Hiding his sense of letdown, Sam checked his watch. "It's late. Why don't we talk again after you've had a chance to think this over?"

She gave a slow nod. "I think that's a good idea. I wish I could give you an answer right now, but…" Her words trailed off.

"I'm asking a lot, Cara. I know that. You need to be sure about whatever you decide. But can I ask you to think about one more thing?" Her hand remained nestled between his, and he hoped that was a good sign. "Reverend Andrews said in his sermon a few weeks ago that good marriages don't happen without a lot of work. I promise you that I'm committed to doing the work this time. I'll never be the world's best communicator, but I promise that I'll never shut you out again. I want to share everything with you, the good and the bad. And I want to grow old with you, sitting on that porch swing at the house as we watch our children…and grandchildren."

Startled, Cara stared at him. "I didn't think you wanted children anymore."

"I told you, my priorities have shifted. When I saw you with Jenna, I realized how much you love children. And what a wonderful mother you'd be. And as I've treated children over the past few months and watched them interact with their parents, I've begun to realize how special the gift of parenthood is. I'd like to share that with you. I was too selfish in the past to understand that the so-called sacrifices of parenthood aren't sacrifices at all, but opportunities to express love."

Cara gave him a searching look. "You can't decide to have children to please someone else, Sam."

He'd been afraid she'd come to that conclusion. But that wasn't his motivation at all. He'd been thinking more and more about the importance of family these past weeks. Yes, he hoped his decision would make her happy. But he was doing it as much for himself as for her. Having children would enrich both their lives…and the lives of their children, he hoped.

"I'm not doing it to please you, Cara. It's what I want, too."

A glimmer of joy sparked to life on her face, but it quickly gave way to a poignant sadness. "We weren't successful years ago, Sam. There's no guarantee we would be now."

"Our lives have changed a great deal. In the past, we were both stressed and overworked. That's not conducive to achieving a pregnancy. It might be different now. And if it doesn't happen, I'm open to adoption."

Tonight had been one surprise after another. The old Sam wouldn't even have considered that option.

"I'll sleep on it," Cara promised.

With a nod, he released her hand and stood. "I think we should call it a night."

He was right. She rose, flipped off the lights and led the way to the kitchen door, locking it behind her. And as Sam followed her to her car, she had a feeling that this was another one of those nights when sleep would be a long time coming.

Wiping a weary hand down his face, Sam turned into his driveway. He'd been in Rolla since early morning, dealing with two crises at the hospital, and now it was twilight. If things were going to go haywire, he wished they'd picked a different week. After his emotional discussion with Cara last night, he'd slept less than three hours. She hadn't seemed to fare much better, given the restless noises he'd heard from her room throughout the night.

He'd just drifted off when the phone rang at six-thirty, summoning him to the hospital. Cara's room had been quiet as he dressed, and he hoped she'd managed to fall asleep at last. He'd left a note for her on the counter, and tried calling when he'd had a couple of quick breaks. But she hadn't answered. Perhaps she'd been out in the garden, he speculated.

As he parked and headed for the house, a sudden, strong gust of warm wind whipped past, and he felt a spattering of rain. The weather service's prediction of a storm seemed to have been accurate, for once. He picked up his pace, noting with surprise that the windows in the house were all dark. Odd. Cara tended to turn on a lot of lights at night.

When he stepped inside and flipped on the kitchen light, apprehension rippled through him. The absolute quiet in the house suggested that no one was home. After calling Cara's name twice without a response, that suspicion was confirmed.

Frowning, he planted his fists on his hips and scanned the counter, thinking she might have left a message for him. But the only note in sight was the one he'd scrawled this morning, shifted into a different position. Yet her car was in the driveway.

With an effort, he held his growing concern in check. There was probably a very good explanation for her absence. She could be with Marge, he reasoned. The two had become good friends. Reaching for the phone, he punched in the number of the inn, needing the reassurance that she was okay. But after three rings, he got the answering machine.

Beyond Marge, he had no idea who else to call. Cara

had become acquainted with a number of people in town, but she'd been too busy with the restaurant opening to cement any real friendships. Her social life was pretty nil at this point.

Frustrated, Sam raked his fingers through his hair. In light of the fact that her car was here, she had to be with someone. Maybe Marge. There was no need to panic. It was only eight o'clock. She could walk through the door any minute.

But by eight-thirty, twilight had given way to darkness and the alarm he was trying to keep in check escalated. It wasn't like Cara to be inconsiderate. During all the years he'd known her, she'd always called if she was going to be delayed, or left a note if she had to run an unexpected errand. She'd done neither tonight. Since she knew he'd be worried by her absence, he couldn't believe that she'd neglect to leave some information about her plans. Unless something was wrong. A wave of panic washed over him, and without further debate he picked up the phone and dialed Dale Lewis's number.

"Sheriff? Sam Martin." A tremor ran through his voice, and he cleared his throat. "Sorry to bother you at home on a Sunday night, but I've been in Rolla most of the day and when I got home half an hour ago Cara was gone. Her car's in the driveway, however. The thing is, it's not like her to wander around at night. Darkness has a tendency to trigger panic attacks."

"Have you checked with any of her friends?"

"I called the inn. Marge is the only person she knows well in town. There's no answer there." A flash of light ricocheted through the house, followed by a crash of thunder. The few drops of rain Sam had felt earlier suddenly turned into a downpour, and his grip on the phone tightened. "I don't want to overreact, but I'm worried about her."

"I understand. Let me put in a few calls and see if there's any news that might have some bearing on this. It could be that…"

As Dale continued to speak, another flash illuminated the room. At first, Sam thought it was lightning again. But this one had followed more of a pattern, he realized. He walked to the front window and lifted the curtain, watching as Cara emerged from Marge's car and dashed toward the house, dodging the rain.

"Sheriff? Looks like it was a false alarm," he interrupted the other man. "Marge just dropped off Cara in front of the house."

"That's good news."

"Sorry I bothered you."

"No problem. That's why I'm here. Don't ever hesitate to call if you have a concern. Good night."

As Sam continued to grip the phone, Cara entered in a gust of wind and rain, pushing the door shut behind her. Droplets of water clung to her fiery hair, and dark splotches of moisture peppered her clothing. When she spotted him in the living room, she shook her head and smiled. "What a night!"

Her lighthearted, carefree tone riled him, and his relief morphed into anger in a heartbeat. Didn't she know that her unexplained absence would wreak havoc with his peace of mind? He didn't even want to think about some of the dire scenarios he'd concocted as he'd paced the house before calling the sheriff.

"Where have you been?"

At his grim face, her smile faltered. "At church. Working on decorations for the seventy-fifth anniversary celebration."

"You might have let me know."

"I left a note."

"Where?"

"On the kitchen table."

"It wasn't there when I got home."

"That's where I left it."

"Do you have any idea how worried I was? I even called the sheriff." He pinned her with an incensed gaze and lifted the phone to illustrate.

His anger snuffed out the last spark of happiness on her face. "I told you, I left a note."

As he took a step toward her, he saw a flash of fear in her eyes. Watched as she took an involuntary step back. Checked his advance as her words began to register. "You left a note?"

"Yes. On the table." Her tone was subdued now. Sad, almost.

Without another word, Sam backtracked to the kitchen. The table was empty. But when he widened his search, he caught sight of the corner of a white sheet of paper peeking out from behind the trash can. Striding across the room, he retrieved it and scanned the scrawled message.

"Sam: Went with Marge to work on decorations for the church's anniversary celebration. Should be home by nine."

Slowly Sam exhaled. The wind must have blown the note off the table when he entered, wedging it between the trash can and the wall. His worry had been for naught. Nor had Cara disregarded his feelings.

Now he had a bigger problem to deal with. A few moments ago, as he'd confronted her in the living room, he'd seen her sudden fear. His outburst must have reminded her of the way he'd behaved after the attack, he realized. She'd told him again, just last night, that he had sometimes frightened her. And that she couldn't live with that fear. For her, uncontrolled anger was a deal breaker.

Closing his eyes, Sam prayed that Cara would realize that his behavior tonight had been driven by concern for her. By love. By fear that she was in trouble. That it was an entirely different kind of anger than the frustrated fury he'd experienced after the attack. Tonight, his anger had been reaction, not rage.

Prepared to plead his case, Sam returned to the living room. But it was empty.

Moving down the hall, he raised his hand and gave a tentative knock on her door. "Cara? I found the note. It must have blown off the table. I'm sorry for getting angry. Can we talk about this?"

The silence stretched so long that Sam wondered if she was going to ignore him. But at last she spoke.

"Not tonight, Sam."

The weariness and resignation in her voice twisted his gut, and he leaned his forehead against her closed door. He'd be willing to beg for her forgiveness, if he thought that would do any good. But actions spoke louder than words, and he'd blown it tonight, as evidenced by Cara's withdrawal.

He could only pray that her retreat wasn't permanent.

Chapter Fifteen

"Now that's a smart move, weeding before the heat becomes too oppressive."

From her kneeling position beside Sam's perennial garden, Cara looked up and shaded her eyes. "Reverend Andrews! This is a surprise." She rose, taking the helping hand he extended, and as she brushed off the knees of her jeans she checked her watch. Eight-thirty. "You're out and about early."

"It's never too early to do the Lord's work."

Curious, she tilted her head and studied him. "Are you here for professional reasons?"

"Partly. But also doing a favor for a friend. Do you have a few minutes?"

"Sure. I know it's more the hour for orange juice, but how about some lemonade on the back porch?"

"I could be tempted."

"At least lemonade is an innocent vice, if you have to have one."

"True." A grin lifted the corners of his mouth. "I'll meet you in back."

A few minutes later, when Cara stepped out onto the porch, she found that the minister had claimed one of the wicker chairs Sam had added a couple of weeks ago. Handing him his drink, she scooted onto the swing.

"I always did like porch swings." He took a sip of his lemonade, the wicker creaking as he leaned back. "We had one when I was a child."

"So did we. Sam put this up not long after I arrived."

"Speaking of Sam...he's why I'm here."

Caution warred with speculation on her face. She hadn't had any contact with Sam since his attempt to talk with her through her closed door last night, and she'd heard him leave far earlier than usual this morning. In a way, she was glad she'd had some time alone. His behavior last night had thrown her, and she'd needed to sort through her reaction.

Her hour in the garden had been enlightening. As she'd weeded, enjoying the warm caress of the sun on her back, she'd come to two conclusions. First, her retreat last night had been a Pavlovian response to Sam's anger. It was what she'd been conditioned to do by experience. She'd reacted, the way a knee jerks by reflex when tapped with a hammer, rather than using critical thinking to analyze what had happened.

Second, when she *had* done some analysis, she'd recognized that Sam's anger had been driven by fear for her safety. He hadn't simply lashed out at her because she was a convenient target, as had been the case in the past.

Nevertheless, the glint of fury in his eyes had

unnerved her. No amount of logic or critical thinking seemed able to mitigate that. It had reminded her too much of the man she'd had to tiptoe around for months, never sure when the next explosion would occur, or what would trigger it.

"What about Sam?" Cara asked, taking a slow sip of her lemonade.

"He stopped by this morning to chat." At her curious expression, the minister smiled. "He's been doing that quite a lot, in fact, since you came to town and he began attending services with you. We've had a number of discussions about faith and the Bible. He asks good questions."

More surprises, Cara reflected. Until yesterday, Sam had accompanied her to every Sunday service, and she'd been praying that his attendance would lead him to a closer relationship with the Lord. In that regard at least, it seemed her prayers had been answered.

"I'm glad to hear that, Reverend."

"Today was a little different, though. He called me at six-thirty and said he had a matter of some urgency to discuss. I met him at church at seven, and we talked for about an hour. He told me his story, Cara. As well as the way he'd like it to end. When we finished, he asked me if I'd drop by to see you."

She swirled the ice in her glass, staring at the opaque liquid. "To plead his case?"

"No. Just to let you know that I'm aware of the history, and that I'm available if you'd like to talk about it."

Tracing her finger around the rim of the tumbler, Cara used one toe to keep the swing moving back and forth in a steady, predictable, soothing motion. "Our relationship has had problems for years, Reverend."

"And they escalated after the attack on Sam."

She gave the minister a cautious look. "Did he tell you about...the waitress?"

"Yes. It's hard to forgive betrayal. Or almost betrayal. And perhaps even harder to learn to trust again. Sam's well aware of that." The minister's manner was conversational and sympathetic, not probing. He didn't push her to confide in him, and for that very reason Cara felt comfortable doing so.

"The funny thing is, I never thought I could do either. But after my own experience with trauma..." She stopped again. "Did he tell you about the shooting I witnessed?"

"No. All he said was that you'd had a harrowing experience of your own not long ago."

"Yes." Cara gave him a brief recap. "As terrible as it was, it did help me better understand how easy it is to lose control over your life—and to see things more from Sam's perspective. And after I came to Oak Hill, it was obvious to me that Sam had changed, that his contrition was real. I prayed about it a lot, and in time my heart began to soften. I started to trust him again. But last night..." Her words trailed off.

"He got angry."

"Very. It reminded me of how bad things were at the end."

"I suppose the difference was that in this case, his anger was prompted by fears for your safety. In fact, I suspect he wasn't so much angry as distraught with worry."

"I realize that now. Still, the incident scared me. I thought I was ready to take the risk of loving him again, but now I'm not sure."

"Haven't you already taken it?"

Jolted, she stared at him. "What do you mean?"

"If you didn't care for him, do you think you'd be agonizing over this decision? You're hesitating because you're afraid of being hurt again. But if you didn't love Sam, you couldn't be hurt, could you? Nor would you consider taking the risk."

That was true, Cara acknowledged. She did love Sam. The ember had never died; it had simply been smoldering deep in her heart. And fueled by Sam's kindness and consideration, it had been fanned to life again. Fear, not love, was the issue.

"You're right. I just need to figure out how to get over being.afraid."

"Do you remember the sermon I gave the first weekend Sam came to services?"

"Yes. I've thought of it often."

"It's hard to beat the Lord's advice, as recorded by John. 'Do not let your hearts be troubled. Trust in God still, and trust in Me.' And Ezekiel has some good advice, too. Chapter eighteen, verses twenty-one and twenty-two. Check it out when you have a minute."

The minister took the last swallow of his lemonade and stood. "You've known Sam a lot longer than I have, Cara. I can only tell you that I'm impressed by his honesty and integrity. My gut tells me that he loves you, and that given a second chance, he'll do his best to build a solid marriage. You'll have to decide whether his sincere intentions are enough to justify the risk you mentioned."

He stuck his hands in the pockets of his slacks and regarded her with a kind expression. "I didn't come to advise you about your decision, but I can caution you about one thing. Don't expect perfection. From either of you. Humans are flawed, and marriages aren't perfect. Yet when both people are committed to making it work, to approaching it in an unselfish and loving manner, it's the closest thing we have on earth to heaven." He held out his hand, and Cara took it. "I'll leave you to your thoughts. But I'm close by if you want to talk some more. And so is the Lord."

As the minister disappeared around the edge of the house, Cara rose and headed for her bedroom to retrieve her Bible. Riffling through the pages, she found the passage in Ezekiel that Reverend Andrews had referenced.

"But if the wicked man turns away from all the sins he committed, if he keeps all my statutes and does what is right and just, he shall surely live, he shall not die. None of the crimes he has committed shall be remembered against him; he shall live because of the virtue he has practiced."

There was a parallel in that passage to Sam, Cara conceded, her expression pensive. Though he hadn't been evil, he had sinned. But he was trying his best to atone for his mistakes, living a virtuous, just life. If the Lord could forgive, if He could reward goodness and promise that no crimes would be remembered against a sinner who'd reformed, how could she do less?

All at once, the direction Cara had been seeking came

to her. And with it, a sense of closure, and of peace. Her hand on the Bible, Cara spoke to the Lord in silent prayer.

Lord, You know that I've always believed that marriage is forever. And I do love Sam. Since we parted, I've felt a void in my life. I knew we had unfinished business, but I had no idea how to tie up the loose ends. Then tragic circumstances brought me here, to his house. I was given the opportunity to witness the changes he's made in his life. To rekindle the love that has lain dormant in my heart all these months. To learn to trust, and to find a way to forgive.

Last night shook my confidence, Lord. But Reverend Andrews is right. And Marge was, too. None of us is perfect. In my heart, I feel You calling me to give our marriage another chance. Please grant me the courage to take that risk, and the wisdom and grace to persevere as we attempt to build a new life together.

Sam pulled his key out of the ignition and let out a weary sigh. He'd slept no more than a couple of hours last night, and risen early to talk to Reverend Andrews. The lack of rest and the unrelenting stress over his relationship with Cara had taken a toll. After finishing with his last patient at five o'clock, he'd been more than ready to call it a day.

Reaching down to the seat beside him, he lifted the bouquet of two dozen long-stemmed red roses. He'd considered calling Cara all day but hadn't followed through. His instincts told him that their next conversation needed to be face-to-face. Except…her car wasn't in the driveway, he realized, noting the empty space where she always parked.

Had she left?

Gone back to Philly?

He vaulted from the car, covering the distance to the back door at close to a sprint. His hand fumbled with the key, more clumsy than usual, and it took him two tries to insert it in the lock.

As he pushed open the door, the first thing he saw was a large note, securely taped on all four sides to the front of the refrigerator.

Sam. Please meet me at the inn.

For a few seconds he stared at the message. Had she moved out? Sought refuge with Marge? Striding down the hall, he threw open her door. Relief coursed through him as he scanned the room, taking in the shoes at the foot of the bed, the brush on the dresser, the blouse draped over the back of a chair. She hadn't left. *Thank you, God!*

On shaky legs he retraced his route to the driveway and slid once more into the car. *Lord, please help me smooth things out*, he prayed as he drove toward the inn. *Don't let me blow this the way I blew it last night.*

Most Mondays were quiet at the inn, and today seemed to be no exception. The place looked deserted when he parked in front. But he'd barely pressed the bell when the door was thrown open by Marge—almost as if she'd been waiting for him. Her eyes twinkled as she scanned the roses.

"Cara left me a note to meet her here." Sam felt warmth creep up his neck and hoped Marge wouldn't notice.

Stepping aside, the innkeeper motioned him in as she reached for her purse. "She's in the dining room. I'm going to St. Louis to visit a friend, and I don't expect to be back until at least nine tomorrow morning. I don't have any guests tonight, either. Make yourself at home." She dug through the side pocket of her purse and withdrew a key, handing it to him as she brushed past. "You might find a use for that later."

With that, she left, pulling the door shut with a decisive click before he could ask for clarification.

Quiet descended after Marge departed. Well, not absolute quiet, he realized as he absently slipped the key into his shirt pocket. Soft classical music played from the vicinity of the dining room. Forcing his unsteady legs forward, he walked down the hall, stopping at the doorway to take in the scene.

A table for two, in the middle of the room, had been set with white linen and silver. Crystal goblets reflected the golden light from the candles that burned in the center. Enticing aromas wafted from the kitchen, and the harp and violin music created a romantic ambience.

Despite the loveliness of the setting, it was Cara who drew his attention when she appeared in the doorway from the kitchen. He'd always considered her beautiful, but she'd never looked more gorgeous than at this moment. Dressed in a black cocktail dress, with spaghetti straps that exposed her shoulders and a skirt that revealed her shapely legs, she was stunning.

His mouth went dry, and his voice deserted him. All he could do was stare, leaving it up to her to break the silence.

"Hi, Sam."

Her husky greeting did nothing to slow his metabolism. While he hadn't been sure what to expect tonight, this hadn't been it.

Clearing his throat, he tried to respond. It came out more like a croak. "Hi."

"The roses are beautiful."

He forced his gaze away from her and stared down. He'd forgotten he was holding them. Moving toward her, he held them out. "They're for you."

She took them, burying her face in the velvety petals as she inhaled. "They smell wonderful. Thank you."

Up close, Sam could see the delicate pink tinge on her cheeks, as well as the sparkle of anticipation in her eyes. While an almost palpable undercurrent of excitement rippled through her, he also sensed an aura of peace. It was an arresting—and encouraging—combination.

"You…you don't look like a chef tonight."

He had no idea where that remark had come from, but the sudden, soft curve of her lips suggested that she found it amusing.

"Thanks. I think. But I did prepare a gourmet meal. I hope you're hungry."

"Sure. Yes." Although he hadn't eaten much all day, food was the last thing on his mind. But it was obvious that Cara had gone to a lot of effort.

"Have a seat while I put these in water." She gestured toward the table and disappeared into the kitchen.

She was back before he had a chance to regroup, setting the roses on a nearby table, and while he did his best to do justice to a cheesy shrimp appetizer and a Caesar salad, Cara kept up a running commentary. He could tell she was nervous, but he was still trying to regain his balance and did little to contribute to the con-versation, letting her take the lead. Only when they were halfway through the filet mignon entrée did he feel steady enough to take advantage of a lull in the conversation and ask the question that was burning a hole in his gut.

Clenching his napkin into a tight ball in his lap, Sam took a deep breath. "Cara, this meal, this—" He motioned around at the setting. "Everything. Does it... does it mean what I think it does?"

She looked down and toyed with her fork, confining her answer to a single soft word. "Yes."

He felt the sting of tears, tears of relief, of joy, of gratitude. Of hope realized, of a wish fulfilled. His throat constricted with emotion, rendering speech impossible. Instead, he took her hand.

For several seconds she stared at the scarred fingers entwined with hers. Like his hand, their hearts had much healing to do. And scars would remain. But just as Sam had gone on to build a new, if different, life, so, too, would they.

Lifting her head, Cara looked at the man she had married. When she saw the sheen of tears in his eyes, her own vision blurred. The old Sam would never have allowed his emotions to show. Such a display would have indicated a loss of control, and vulnerability. The new Sam, however, seemed willing to take that risk, to share with her, to trust her with his heart. Just as she was willing to trust him with hers.

"The fact is, Sam, I never stopped loving you." Her words were as soft and gentle as a lover's caress. "But I was afraid of being hurt again. I didn't think anything could convince me to give our relationship another chance. Then I ended up here. And I saw for myself how you've changed. I realized that you were sincere about wanting to start over, and I believe that you're committed now to making our marriage work. I prayed about it a lot. And in the end, I couldn't walk away. I love you too much. I always have."

When her voice broke on the last word, he squeezed her fingers. "I love you, too. With all my heart."

He rose and reached for her hands, pulling her up beside him as gratitude and adoration suffused his face. He might never be the most verbal man, but even without words, Cara could see that she was cherished and loved with a devotion that took her breath away.

When he lowered his head to claim her lips, Cara's arms went around him, his strong shoulders and broad back familiar beneath her fingers as she melted into his embrace and gave herself to his kiss. It felt good in his arms. And right.

It felt like coming home.

When Sam at last drew back, he searched her face, drinking in the familiar features that had brightened his life since the day they met…and filled his dreams while they were apart. After their unexpected kiss a week ago, doubt and fear had flickered across her face, leaving him filled with a wrenching uncertainty about the outcome. Tonight he saw a glow of happiness, a contentment and serenity, that wiped away any lingering apprehension. The ending he'd prayed for had been given to him. Cara was home at last.

Pressing her cheek to his chest with a hand that wasn't quite steady, he rested his chin on her soft hair and stroked her back, enjoying the feel of her in arms that had been empty for too long. As empty as his heart. And he marveled at her willingness to forgive and to trust again, after all his mistakes. It was a precious gift that he would thank God for every day of his life.

He could have stayed like that for hours, but after a few moments she eased back slightly. "Whatever is in your pocket is leaving a permanent impression in my cheek," she teased, her voice a bit husky.

Puzzled, he fished around until his fingers encountered the forgotten key. He withdrew it and held it out for her inspection. "Marge gave me this when I arrived. She said I might want to use it later, but I have no idea what it's for. She left before I could ask her."

Backing up a little more within the circle of his arms, Cara read the tag that was attached to the key. When soft color suffused her cheeks, Sam tipped her chin up with a gentle finger and gave her a quizzical look. "What is it?"

"It's for the Rose Room."

That didn't mean a thing to him. "Why would she give it to me?"

Her color deepened. "It…it's the honeymoon suite."

A soft chuckle rumbled deep in Sam's chest. "Marge, a closet romantic? Who would have guessed?" Then his eyes darkened and he stroked her cheek. "She also told me she'd be gone until tomorrow morning. And that no one else is staying at the inn tonight."

Cara tilted her head and looked at him, a smile whispering at her mouth. "We haven't had dessert yet."

His slow, answering smile warmed her from the tips of her toes to the top of her ears. "I think that's what the key is for."

Stepping back, he held out his hand in invitation. He couldn't think of a better way to seal their renewed commitment. He prayed Cara would agree.

She didn't disappoint him. Without hesitation, she placed her fingers in his.

And as he drew her toward the grand staircase, Cara recalled a remark Reverend Andrews had made earlier in the day. He'd said that when two people are committed to making marriage work, when they approach it in an unselfish and loving manner, it's the closest thing we have on earth to heaven.

That's what she was determined to create with Sam. Heaven on earth. And she knew he felt the same way.

She knew something else, as well. With their renewed commitment, with faith in God's loving care and endless grace, they would succeed. And together they would build a bright and shining future from the ashes of their past.

Epilogue

"**Y**ou lucked out with the weather, Cara. August can be a sauna in Missouri. The balmy temperature must be a good sign." As Marge flicked a minuscule speck of lint off Cara's teal-green, short-sleeved silk suit, the innkeeper smiled. "My, you look lovely. As pretty as any bride."

Surveying herself in the full-length mirror set in an ornate Victorian frame in the Rose Room, Cara had to admit that she did look like a bride. She might not be attired in the traditional white gown she'd worn when she and Sam were wed, but the soft blush of color in her cheeks and the sparkle in her eyes was the same as it had been on their wedding day.

"I feel like a bride."

"You should. A vow renewal is a very special occasion. And I'm honored you chose to have the ceremony here."

"The inn will always be a special place for me, Marge. And for Sam. We didn't consider doing it anywhere else."

"It will also be your second home soon, if reservations continue to pour in at the rate they did this past week. Now that the word is spreading that you've signed on for a permanent gig, I can't keep up with the calls. I took a reservation this morning for December."

"The response has been gratifying."

"And well deserved. You'll be a great asset to Oak Hill, Cara. And I don't mean only because of the restaurant."

On impulse, Cara leaned over and gave the innkeeper a hug, doing her best not to inhale any of the wispy feathers from the shocking-pink boa Marge had draped over the sparkly, multicolored tunic and black satin pants she'd donned in honor of the occasion.

"Thank you for everything, Marge. Including the good advice about love."

"You're welcome." She patted Cara's back, then pulled away and sniffled. "Goodness. You'll have me blubbering like a baby in a minute."

Plucking a nosegay of cream-colored roses nestled in tulle off the marble-topped dresser, she handed it to Cara. "Okay, I think we're set. Reverend Andrews is waiting in the gazebo. Abby Warner is set to take a picture for the *Gazette*. There's a luscious-looking cake in the dining room from that great Danish bakery that Dr. Martin favors. And speaking of the good doctor, I left him pacing in the foyer, waiting for his bride in the honored tradition of all nervous grooms. Are you ready?"

"Yes."

Marge opened the door, stepping back to allow Cara to precede her.

When Cara reached the top of the grand staircase, she paused. As Marge had indicated, Sam was pacing in the inn's grand foyer. He was dressed in an impeccable dark gray suit that emphasized his broad shoulders, a cream-colored rose in his lapel. A navy blue tie with a subtle teal-colored pattern lay against his crisp white shirt, and gold cuff links caught the light at his wrists. The word *handsome* didn't come close to doing him justice.

But when he stopped and looked up, it was his eyes that held her mesmerized. Filled with love, gratitude, adoration—they held everything a bride could ever hope to see in her groom. Emotion tightened her throat, and she smiled down at him.

As Cara began her descent, Sam had to remind himself to breathe. Backlit by the stained-glass window on the landing, her glorious hair looked for all the world like a halo. The slender skirt and fitted jacket emphasized her trim figure, and there was a radiance—and joy—about her that seeped deep into his soul and illuminated it.

No longer did he have to rely on dreams to fill the lonely place in his heart.

His dreams had come true.

When she reached the bottom of the stairs, he held out his hands and she placed hers inside.

"You look beautiful." He tugged her a bit closer, but as he leaned down Marge interrupted.

"Now, now, Dr. Martin. Time for that after the ceremony. We have pictures to take and vows to renew. Abby, where's Jason?"

As Sam whispered "later" in her ear, Cara drew back, and Abby Warner stepped out of the shadows where she'd discreetly melted while the tender scene unfolded.

"On another photo assignment in Rolla. I'm doing

double duty today." The *Gazette* editor turned to Cara and Sam. "I hope you don't mind if we run a picture, but this is as close to a society wedding as Oak Hill is likely to get. Town doctor and world-class chef…that's big news here."

"It will be good for business, too," Marge chimed in.

"Of course we don't mind," Cara assured Abby, giving Sam's hand a squeeze. "Where would you like us?"

"How about on the steps, under the art glass window on the landing? That will make a dramatic picture."

As Sam and Cara complied, Marge watched with an indulgent grin.

Sixty seconds later, Abby gave them a wistful smile and tucked her camera back in its case. "That will do it. My best wishes to you both. I can let myself out, Marge." With a wave, she headed for the front door.

As it closed behind her, Cara angled toward the inn-keeper, curious about the brief, melancholy yearning she'd caught in the editor's eyes. "Is Abby married, Marge?"

"Just to that newspaper, I'm sorry to say. She'd make the right man a fine wife, but the *Gazette* has always come first in her heart. That's the blessing—and the curse—of a family legacy, I suppose. She doesn't have a minute to call her own, let alone think about romance."

"Been there, done that." Sam joined in the conversation, taking Cara's hand and looking at her as he spoke. "And I never intend to do it again."

"Good for you. I like a man who has his priorities straight. And now I believe you two have a date with a minister."

She led the way to the back of the house and pushed

open the door. "The garden is yours. I'll ice down the champagne and leave it in the dining room."

"You can still come if you like, Marge," Cara said.

"No, my dear, this is your private moment. Yours and Sam's, to share with the Lord. No other witnesses are necessary."

Sam crooked his elbow, and when Cara slipped her hand through he covered it with his own. As they walked through the old-fashioned garden, among hollyhocks and roses and zinnias, he smiled at her. "I suspect she'll peek through the upstairs window."

"I do, too. She's a romantic at heart. Do you mind?"

"No. I only have eyes for you, anyway."

Smiling, he led her toward the elaborate, white-lattice Victorian gazebo, his grip tightening as they approached.

"Nervous?" She shot him a teasing look.

"No." His response was quick and confident, and there was no trace of levity in his expression as they ascended the wooden steps to renew the vows that bound them together. "Today is the answer to all my prayers."

Hers, too, Cara acknowledged, as they joined hands and faced each other in front of Reverend Andrews. For in Sam's dear blue eyes she saw a love as deep and as rich and as true as her own. A love that would sustain them for better, for worse. For richer, for poorer. In sickness and in health.

All the days of their lives.

* * * * *

Dear Reader,

From This Day Forward launches my new miniseries, HEARTLAND HOMECOMINGS, for Steeple Hill. All of the books are set in the fictional town of Oak Hill, Missouri, and all feature dramatic, compelling stories about characters who face daunting challenges.

In this book Sam must rebuild a shattered career as he endeavors to win back the love of his estranged wife, while Cara copes with a trauma of her own as she struggles with forgiveness. Reconciliation, trust and the redeeming power of love—and faith—are key themes as these two special people are reunited in America's heartland.

Come February please watch for the second book in the series, *A Dream To Share,* in which Abby Warner wages the battle of her life as she fights to hold on to her family's publishing legacy.

Finally, I invite you to visit my Web site at www.irenehannon.com for all my latest news.

May the upcoming holiday season be filled with joy, laughter and love for each of you!

Irene Hannon

QUESTIONS FOR DISCUSSION

1. In *From This Day Forward,* the couple's estrangement begins long before the attack on Sam, when ambition causes them both to put their careers first. Why did this hurt their marriage? Had Sam not been attacked, do you think their relationship would have survived? Why or why not?

2. Cara's friend, Liz, contacts Sam for help without Cara's knowledge. At first Cara thinks Liz has betrayed her, but later accepts that her friend acted out of love. Have you ever faced a situation where someone you cared about needed help but couldn't acknowledge it? How did you handle it? How did the other person react to what you did?

3. When they first get back together, Sam is surprised to find that Cara still prays after all that's happened. She responds that she's more inclined to pray now, and he counters that he's less inclined to. Discuss the reasons for the disparity in their approach to prayer. In times of distress are you more or less inclined to pray? Why?

4. Sam's difficulty communicating is evidenced by his inability to connect with his patients. What are the hallmarks of good communication? Discuss some passages in the book where good communication skills are demonstrated. Why are they effective?

5. After Sam's world falls apart, he begins to understand what really matters in life. Why does it often take traumatic events to force people to sort out their priorities? What can we do to ensure that we never lose sight of the most important things?

6. When Cara is confronted with Sam's apparent unfaithfulness, her trust is shattered. Why is it more difficult to forgive unfaithfulness than many other transgressions? How can trust be rebuilt in a situation like that? What guidance does the Bible offer?

7. After Cara arrives in Oak Hill, what are some of the nonverbal ways Sam lets her know that he cares about her and wants to make amends? Are actions more or less important than words in conveying how we feel about someone? Why?

8. When Cara comes to Oak Hill, she finds a changed man. What did Sam learn in the months after the attack that helped him rebuild his life? What does he learn in the course of the book?

9. After witnessing the murder, Cara suffers from debilitating panic attacks and post-traumatic stress disorder. Have you ever experienced a fear or phobia that affected your life? How did you deal with it? Did your faith play a role?

10. Cara is afraid that the changes in Sam won't last. Do you think people can change as dramatically as Sam did? What is necessary for those changes to endure?

INTRODUCING

Love Inspired.
HISTORICAL
A NEW TWO-BOOK SERIES.

Every month, acclaimed
inspirational authors
will bring you engaging stories
rich with romance, adventure
and faith set in a variety
of vivid historical times.

*History begins on **February 12**
wherever you buy books.*

Steeple
Hill®

Love Inspired®

REQUEST YOUR FREE BOOKS!

2 FREE INSPIRATIONAL NOVELS
PLUS 2
FREE
MYSTERY GIFTS

YES! Please send me 2 FREE Love Inspired® novels and my 2 FREE mystery gifts. After receiving them, if I don't wish to receive any more books, I can return the shipping statement marked "cancel." If I don't cancel, I will receive 4 brand-new novels every month and be billed just $3.99 per book in the U.S., or $4.74 per book in Canada, plus 25¢ shipping and handling per book and applicable taxes, if any*. That's a savings of 20% off the cover price! I understand that accepting the 2 free books and gifts places me under no obligation to buy anything. I can always return a shipment and cancel at any time. Even if I never buy another book from Steeple Hill, the two free books and gifts are mine to keep forever.

113 IDN EF26   313 IDN EF27

Name	(PLEASE PRINT)	
Address		Apt. #
City	State/Prov.	Zip/Postal Code

Signature (if under 18, a parent or guardian must sign)

Order online at www.LoveInspiredBooks.com

Or mail to Steeple Hill Reader Service™:

IN U.S.A.: P.O. Box 1867, Buffalo, NY 14240-1867
IN CANADA: P.O. Box 609, Fort Erie, Ontario L2A 5X3

Not valid to current Love Inspired subscribers.

Want to try two free books from another series?
Call 1-800-873-8635 or visit www.morefreebooks.com

* Terms and prices subject to change without notice. NY residents add applicable sales tax. Canadian residents will be charged applicable provincial taxes and GST. This offer is limited to one order per household. All orders subject to approval. Credit or debit balances in a customer's account(s) may be offset by any other outstanding balance owed by or to the customer. Please allow 4 to 6 weeks for delivery.

Your Privacy: Steeple Hill is committed to protecting your privacy. Our Privacy Policy is available online at www.eHarlequin.com or upon request from the Reader Service. From time to time we make our lists of customers available to reputable firms who may have a product or service of interest to you. If you would prefer we not share your name and address, please check here. ☐

LIREG07

Love Inspired®

TITLES AVAILABLE NEXT MONTH

Don't miss these four stories in December

A DROPPED STITCHES CHRISTMAS by Janet Tronstad
A special Steeple Hill Café novel in Love Inspired

For Carly Winston, telling her friends the truth about her home life was a huge step. But playing Mary in the local Nativity play gave her courage she never thought she'd have. And spending time with grill owner Randy Parker made her feel like a star.

A HOLIDAY TO REMEMBER by Jillian Hart
A Tiny Blessings Tale

Memories of wartime held former soldier Jonah Fraser captive. Yet single mom Debra Watson gave him a reason to smile for the first time since returning from Iraq. With a matchmaking teen on the job, this was sure to be a holiday he'd never forget.

HEART OF THE FAMILY by Margaret Daley
Fostered by Love

Why didn't big-hearted social worker Hannah Smith like him? Dr. Jacob Hartman couldn't figure it out, but Hannah's dedication to foster children touched his heart. If only he could find a way to get to hers.

THE HEALING PLACE by Leigh Bale

Dr. Emma Shields was Mark Williams's last hope to heal his little girl. And Emma was determined not to let their past history or her own heartbreaking loss stand in the way of a cure. With faith she'd find a way.

LICNM1107